CARL R. PROFFER

The Widows
of Russia

AND OTHER WRITINGS

Ardis, Ann Arbor

Copyright © 1987 by Ardis Publishers
All rights reserved under International and
Pan-American Copyright Conventions
Printed in the United States of America

First paperback edition 1992

Ardis Publishers
2901 Heatherway
Ann Arbor, Michigan 48104

Library of Congress Cataloging-in-Publication Data

Proffer, Carl R.
The Widows of Russia & other essays

1. Russian literature— History and criticism—
Addresses, essays, lectures. I. Title.
PG2933.P76 1987 813'.54 84-20397
ISBN 0-679-74262-X (alk. paper)
CIP

Distributed by Vintage Books,
a division of Random House, Inc.

Contents

Carl Proffer, May 1984. Photo: Wayne Robart.

Introduction

The circumstances of the writing of most of these pieces require some explanation. The memoirs in this book are written not by a septuagenarian looking back over a long life, but by a man of forty-five who knew that he had no more than a year left to live.

Carl had saved notes and diaries from the beginning of his career, planning some day to write at leisure about his life in Russian literature. When he was unexpectedly diagnosed as being in the terminal stages of cancer in 1982, he decided that he would try to do part of this work before he died. There is often a feeling of anger in these articles, introductions and memoirs, easily traced to the effects of five operations in two years, radical monthly chemotherapy (he often wrote while lying on the chemo table), and the pain of knowing he would leave life long before he was ready. But this is only part of the explanation—some of the articles were written years before his illness. Carl went to the Soviet Union for long stays in 1962 and 1969, and visited on the average of once a year until 1979, when he became *persona non grata* and was routinely denied a visa as punishment for his role as publisher of the *Metropole* anthology. In 1969 there was still much hope for change in Russia; ten years later it appeared to Carl that the Brezhnev era demanded nothing less than the destruction of a once-great culture. The years had taken a toll on his friends: some had their careers brutally ruined, some were exiled, others were sent to prison, or died in terrible circumstances. It was a period of complete disillusionment, and based on what he had seen of the real power structure, Carl was skeptical about the possibility of real change, although he never gave up hope. He would be happy at even the minor changes which have come to the Soviet Union since his death, and he would say that Russia should know her past, a difficult thing in a country where writing history is such an unrewarding activity. And this book presents a part of that history as reflected in the literary world.

That a midwestern basketball player turned Slavist would find himself in the position of actually affecting the cultural life of the Soviet Union in a small but measurable way was one of the paradoxes which Carl's Russian friends loved to ponder. He was not of Slavic background, he was no world-traveller, he was not interested in languages until the day he happened on the Russian alphabet, and he did not have any real curiosity about literature until he was in college. All of this made him an exotic in the Moscow-Leningrad literary milieu—which he knew, and certainly used to his advantage when possible. Beginning as a scholar and professor, then as an editor and publisher, Carl gave twenty years of his formidable energy to the cause of Russian literature. He co-founded the publishing house Ardis in 1971, and was the main force behind *Russian Literature Triquarterly*, begun in the same year.

In many ways Ardis is more valued in Russia than it is here, but it would not be wrong to say that before its founding much of Russian literature of the twentieth century remained untranslated, many of the main works of twentieth-century Russian literature had been out of print in Russian for some thirty years, and very few purely literary works were published abroad in Russian by writers still in the Soviet Union. Ardis dealt with all of these issues almost from its inception, and changed the face of Russian literature studies. It provided a place to publish in both Russian and English for writers still in the Soviet Union who did not wish to deal with Western publishers who were overtly political. In some inexplicable way, Ardis became a safe place to publish until the *Metropole* affair. Carl did not do all of this alone by any means, but he was the heart, the energy at the center. Without him it would not have happened. He was the reason such an uncommercial enterprise could come into being with no outside funding (except for the occasional loan from family and friends), and continue to survive.

Carl loathed the cultural bureaucracy of Russia, but the depth of his feeling for its people and literature is on every page of this book, and that love was returned. When news of his illness reached Russia via broadcasts, calls and letters, he received hundreds of telegrams, letters and calls, many from unknown people, such as the readers in Siberia who had once gotten an Ardis book to read for the night, and the woman in Leningrad who wrote that a mass had been said for him, ordered by people he had never met. All of this touched him greatly.

Many of the pieces collected here were written in the eight months before Carl's death. They are not cast in his customary elegant high style, but are, instead, deliberately uncharming. In dying he wanted to tell the truth as it appeared to him in the most straightforward way possible, without the temporizing those who love Russia often resort to—he did not have to worry about getting another visa. I have edited this book as little as necessary, in respect for the author's wish that it not be smoothed out too much. It is not, however, the book he planned: chapters on other friends (Trifonov, the Kopelevs, Iskander, Voinovich, Aksyonov, Sokolov and many others) were not finished, and the section on Joseph Brodsky was left out at the request of the subject. Nevertheless, as it stands, it is a very special work, written by a man who would want to be remembered not only as a teacher, scholar and publisher, but as a father to four children, and, not so incidentally, my husband.

Ellendea Proffer
February, 1987

The Widows of Russia

Nadezhda Mandelstam. Photo: Wayne Robart.

Nadezhda Mandelstam

Getting to her place was always difficult. Her apartment was located in the New Cheryomushkin ("Bird Cherry") area, which was strewn with clusters of the ugly new pre-fab apartment buildings that ring all of Moscow. Although they wouldn't admit it, cab drivers from the center seldom had even an abstract notion of how to find a major street like Bolshaya Cheryomushkinskaya. Eventually we memorized the long route out Lenin Avenue to Union St. and so on, and at N. M.'s request—she feared having the presence of foreigners made so obvious—we usually had the cab stop a short distance away from her building. It was one of three identical high-rise "towers" (her term) located along a trolley car line (but there were no direct trolleys or buses from the city center, so we always went by taxi). One had to cross the trolley tracks on a very rough entrance drive, which destroyed the cars that used it, and walk around behind the building to get to her entrance. The entrance itself was very dark and, like most floor-level entrances to Moscow apartments, smelled slightly of sewer and garbage. A door to the left of a little elevator opened into a hall which led to her apartment.

Very uncertain that we were in the right place, we rang her bell for the first time at about 3:30 on the afternoon of March 17, 1969. As would always be the case, there was a long wait, then a shuffling of feet, a partial unlocking, a voice asking us to identify ourselves and then a final unlocking. The small old lady stepped aside to admit us, directing us to the kitchen.

Her apartment consisted of an entrance hall—with bathroom and toilet doors directly to the right—and two real rooms ahead: her bedroom through the left-hand door and kitchen through the right. Both of these rooms faced out onto the street and the trolley tracks.

13

The kitchen was roughly 7' x 14' (arms outspread, I could almost touch both walls) and the bedroom 12' x 17'. Although the building was fairly new, everything already looked old and battered. During our early visits we saw her almost exclusively in the kitchen; later when she took to her bed (for the first time in May 1972), we talked to her there. The kitchen was furnished with a small gas range and refrigerator, an unsteady table, a couple of wobbly slat folding chairs, a couple of primitive three-legged stools, and, in the corner by the window, an old high-backed, thin-cushioned wooden settee where she and Ellendea usually sat. (Inge Morath's photo of this period shows her on this settee.) The bedroom was sparsely furnished too: a bed, a couple of tables and lamps, a small low chest, a desk and an armchair. On the walls were paintings by Vaisberg and Birger, among others—all hung, in the Russian style, very high. The plug-in telephone was moved from room to room as convenience dictated, but usually ended up in the bedroom. Vases full of dried flowers, cattails, etc. were always in the bedroom. Bare bulbs and bare wood floors did nothing to lend warmth to the place. N. M. recognized that it was uncomfortable, but said that it had taken working her whole life to get even this in retirement—and it had running water and other things she had done without much of her life, so while she scorned its style, she was glad to have it. Since leaving her father's home, she had never really had a place of her own, a true "home." During her life with Osip Mandelstam finding a room, never mind an apartment, had been difficult. Her time spent teaching in various provincial schools had been no less nomadic, so this apartment was the summit of her material accomplishments. By Soviet standards it was not bad for its genre, but then most of the apartments we were familiar with in Moscow would be considered poverty level in a normal American city.

N. M. said that the apartment had another real virtue—it was usually quiet, in spite of the trolley. But, she complained, she didn't like the summers because when the weather got warmer, it got noisier outside. Cold and snow muffled everything in the winter, and she liked. that. She hated May Day, for example, not only because of the noise of the celebration, but also for its association with the arrest of Mandelstam. At least she was not in some horrendous communal apartment with squabbles in the kitchen and squalor in a shared toilet. The main noises, and she probably didn't notice them, were her own heavy breathing and the tick of her beloved cuckoo clock, announcing the quarter hours relentlessly.

N. M. was not much of a housekeeper, but she maintained a

surface cleanliness. We were already used to the relative poverty in which most Russians live but were still depressed to see her straitened circumstances. No matter how poor, all the Russians we ever knew would go out of their way to make sure the table was ready with food and drink for their guests. N. M.'s table was always meager—for the simple reason that she was poor. Even though she did not complain, I don't think she liked the situation at all or that she was indifferent to "fine" things. In any event, of all the writers we knew, she was the poorest—and had been poor the longest—and this was a continuation of her life with Osip Mandelstam. In the same way, the literary widows whose husbands had not been officially in disfavor during their lifetimes stayed comfortably placed after their deaths. What we had that first day was typical: the world's strongest tea, which she always poured into large unmatched mugs with half an inch of tea leaves in the bottom and a lot floating in the hot water she added to them; some sugar in a bowl; a little bread, cheese, and perhaps butter.

N. M. accompanied this tea—and all conversation—by chain smoking Belomor cigarettes (*papirosy*), a brand named in honor of the White Sea Canal built by slave labor (and with great fanfare) under Stalin in the thirties. She called the tobacco "shit from burial mounds," in memory of those who died building that canal. She smiled when she first pointed out a blackened pot on her shelves—this pot was the "historical archive" in which many of Mandelstam's poems had been saved from confiscation. The smile was revealing: not exactly proud, but not just matter-of-fact either.

We had been recommended to N. M. by a trusted friend, Clarence Brown, the well-known Mandelstam scholar. During our first visit N. M. seemed to be playing the role of poet's widow a bit. However, at this point we did not have a very good sense of who she or Mandelstam were and did not ask the usual sorts of questions, so she saw that she could be more informal. We knew O. M. mainly from a few poems we had read in graduate school, and for us all of the writers of that period (early twentieth century) were as much dead classics as Dostoevsky or Tolstoi. Partly because of our own youth and inexperience it had never before occurred to us how close these writers were to being our contemporaries, of "our age," and that people who actually knew them—even lived with them—were still alive. Thus, as the afternoon wore on and N. M. kept telling stories about anyone we named, we became more and more fascinated and excited.

N. M. seemed to have known every writer we mentioned. Perhaps most stunning to us was that she had known Blok and had frequented the Symbolist and Futurist night clubs (such as the Stray Dog). She was remembering a time that we knew only from books. We kept asking questions, and she kept amazing us—not just by the very fact of her stories, but by the truculent independence of her opinions about all the personalities and events that we knew exclusively from the outdated books typical of Slavic studies. (Bear in mind that her books had not yet been published—and much of what she told us was already in her manuscript which would not be printed until 1970 in New York.)

She was bright and touching, good-humored and bitter at the same time. When she condemned someone, it was usually in a matter-of-fact way; real bitterness only came out when she talked about the things done to O. M. For example, we asked about Isaac Babel, repeating the accepted Western view of him as having the sensitivity of the narrator of his *Red Cavalry*. She laughed and said that the real Babel was quite different, although one could deduce it from his work if one read it in a very special way. She thought him brilliant, clever—and cautious. His curiosity was what led him down strange paths, specifically to Cheka executions which he watched upon the personal invitations of his friends among the secret police. She did not seem especially horrified by this, but was rather sad about it. Since Babel had never done anything against Mandelstam, this was all kept out of the memoirs. On several occasions she mentioned the ways in which the Revolution and the Civil War could affect people who were in a sense thrilled by the violence and blood-lust.

She asked us a lot of questions too—about America, about how we came to be in Moscow, and about our personal lives. She was greatly taken with Ellendea's looks and style. She liked people who spoke their minds just as she did. We felt some kind of mutual attraction from the start. N. M. seemed to like it that we were not of Russian descent, but were in love with Russian culture only for its own sake and that we were not Mandelstam specialists. She liked the divorces in our backgrounds and insisted that second marriages were much better. She was so intrigued by all this personal detail that she even forgave us our lack of interest in religion—she said "later on" we would come to understand. We would learn the importance of God and religion, she said, insisting that "everything that happened here [Russia] happened because of that." At this time there were few external signs of religion in the apartment, but her belief in Orthodoxy was already clear.

On our second visit to her we brought her a Russian Bible, provided by Roger Harrison, a Baptist minister who was currently the Embassy pastor. Roger had a large cache of these forbidden books, often carried under some old clothing in the trunk of his red Barracuda hatchback. Roger told us that the main reason one Scandinavian exchange student was thrown out by the Soviets that spring was that he had been passing out Bibles; after that incident even Roger was more discreet about transporting them. N. M. could not understand why we nonbelievers would take the trouble to run the risk of getting a Bible for her—but she appreciated it very much. Certainly of all the practical gifts we brought during this first series of visits, she appreciated the Bibles (we brought others) more than anything else. She said that the first one was for a Bible *scholar* who had done all of his work without ever actually owning a Bible himself.

Our first two-hour visit to N. M. on St. Patrick's Day in 1969 ended with an invitation to come back again another afternoon. She liked to speak English, but complained about my soft voice and Ellendea's fast tempo. During this initial meeting we had switched back and forth from English to Russian, a practice that continued for several years. As her health and hearing disintegrated, we spoke mostly Russian. But she almost always wrote to us in English, and she was very hard on herself when she realized she was making mistakes. In her very first letter from November 1969 she ended, "Beg pardon for spelling mistakes . . . 70 years old and illiterate . . ." She liked doing things well.

The young Bohemian artist could still be felt in N. M. in 1969. One presumes that in her hot youth she didn't care much about her external surroundings or about what people thought when she used shocking language to say the rather shocking things which she enjoyed saying. (Most of the old Russian women we knew, and most of the not-so-old, would have cringed or run away at the salty language N. M. used.) She still had traces in her of "Nadenka," the young art student who went to bed with Mandelstam the first time they met.

Her interest in art remained. She loved talking about Tyshler and other artists from the teens and twenties. Well-known contemporary Russian artists such as Vladimir Vaisberg and Boris Birger were among her special visitors. We had the impression that she liked setting the two against each other. She had a white-on-white painting by Vaisberg on her bedroom wall when we first visited and made a point of taking us in to look at it. We soon met Birger, who somewhat later on painted a portrait of N. M. which she supposedly didn't like very much, because it had what some saw as a witch-like quality in it. We liked it, however.

It is telling that the only social function that N. M. invited us to attend with her was an art exhibition. It was the first major exhibit of Natalia Severtsova's painting, only the second of her life—she was in her late sixties or early seventies. The exhibit was held in one room and a corridor of the Architecture School just down the street from the Lenin Library. It was shown here rather than in one of the regular galleries as a sign from above that she was not officially accepted as an artist.

On that April day in 1969 when N. M. led us into the exhibit, we saw why Severtsova was not in a state-run gallery. Her works were done in a primitive style—bordering on the surreal in detail. Her marvelous sense of humor was not likely to please artistic solid citizens. She had lots of Russian *cherti* (devils), Soviet bathhouse and wedding scenes, but most of it done ironically. The bathhouse women were grotesquely fat and repulsive. Adam and Eve stood by a seven-branched tree—the couple wearing huge, ugly Soviet watches. A Soviet family portrait was in the same vein, closer to emigre artist David Miretsky's surreal world than to Soviet standards. Her old man in a hut could have been socially sentimentalized, but instead he was keeping company with a bottle of vodka. The people who came liked it as much as we did, and the comment book on the table contained only praise.

N. M. suggested we tell Severtsova (who was an old friend) that if such an exhibit appeared in the United States it would arouse great interest. Since we considered it true, it was easy to say it to the painter. Severtsova was simultaneously pleased and torn by our compliment, since, she said, it could never happen. On the other hand she became nervous when N. M. conveyed to her our wish to buy something. "I'm unofficial," she said apologetically. After thinking it over, she said she was willing to sell, but not anything that "they" might consider negative, like the family portrait. She didn't seem precisely afraid, but simply made it clear right away that she could not do what she liked.

On this occasion Nadezhda Yakovlevna, who usually wore an ugly housedress when we visited, was dressed very well. She wore a long dark wool skirt with a nice sweater and a scarf draped dashingly around her neck. Ellendea said it was chic and very definitely showed the artist in her. N. M. was very calm and self-assured on this occasion and enjoyed showing us around, pointing out what was interesting in these works. We did not know much of this side of her, and we would not see her outside her apartment again until 1977, when she would again show her public persona.

N. M. had taken us to Severtsova's exhibit as a sign of favor, but it was only after we had made a number of other visits that she invited us to a social evening at her place. Among other things, she said she hoped to introduce us to the artists Vaisberg and Birger.

That evening was our first look at N. M.'s real "salon." A dozen or so people arrived and soon there was no place to sit. People wandered back and forth from bedroom to kitchen, and the bottles of wine and vodka we brought soon disappeared. Raisa Orlova later recalled N. M.'s evenings of this time, saying they attracted the best minds, the most talented artists, writers, theologians, priests and philosophers. We did not know this since we were blissfully uninitiated—although Clarence had said we would enjoy her world. That first evening those in attendance included Birger (whose complete *Catalogue* we would publish a few years later, and whose paintings hang in some of the most distinguished collections in Europe); Andrei Sergeev, translator of Robert Frost, T. S. Eliot and others; and Lev Kopelev and Raisa Orlova, both well-known literary critics and an integral part of the dissident world.

It was an evening full of "Russian conversations" on topics which soon aroused passions. One of these was the value of Ukrainian poetry—and Ukrainian culture in general. There was a bitter argument between Lev Kopelev, who was born and brought up in the Ukraine and who to this day is very patriotic about Ukrainian culture, and Sergeev, who despised what he termed "provincial" literatures, and who very snottily made arguments along the lines of Ukrainian not even being a real language. Voices quickly rose, and if it had not been for the distinguished company, they would have at least been swearing at each other. The argument ended suddenly in fuming silence from both parties. Sergeev came off as a bantam rooster attacking the charismatic Kopelev just for the sake of making an impression.

N. M. liked Sergeev very much, partly because of the Eliot translation, I imagine, and he was a great collector of first editions, including Mandelstam. She told us that if we met anyone in Moscow now, before we dealt with them very much we should go to Sergeev, and he would tell us if the person was a "good person" or a "bad person." We did in fact ask him for help, and he did warn us in one or two cases.

So it was that we first witnessed the Soviet salon phenomenon, and discovered that each circle had at least one kind of "security" officer to keep out informers. Which brings me to the subject of N. M. and fear in general. From the first meeting we were struck by her fear. She told us that when Clarence Brown first came to see her, she hid behind a

19

closed door at Akhmatova's, afraid to show herself. She frequently mentioned the possibility of her arrest. We tried to talk her out of this, but she always insisted, as with many things, that we simply "didn't understand." She often peered out the front windows after we arrived, checking to see if we were being followed. As each book came out, her level of fear went up. But she was not arrested until after her death.

N. M. was afraid from beginning to end. But in this she was like her countrymen—and there were good reasons for this. Repeatedly during our six-month stay in 1969 we had the jarring experience of going to a new home, asking about a photograph on a wall or table, and getting the answer: that's my father, he was shot in 1937. (The relation and year might change, but the formula and the shock were always the same.) Yes, we agreed, this was the kind of thing that could make one afraid for a long time. For that matter we were usually afraid ourselves, often so much so that we had stomach pains for days, caused by the stories we were hearing and by the illegal things we were doing—such as getting and giving away large numbers of books, including especially dangerous ones such as the Russian *Doctor Zhivago,* Solzhenitsyn's novels, Orwell, Bibles, and so on. Arrests and searches of foreign students were common: one exchange couple was sent out of the USSR after the KGB picked the wife up on the street. Fear was logical even for us, so why shouldn't N. M. and so many others be afraid after the carnivorous age they had been through.

In N. M.'s case fear was especially understandable. In 1969 the official attitude to Solzhenitsyn was rapidly changing and rumors of punishment were in the air. N. M.'s first volume of memoirs was already in the pipeline to appear *abroad.* Both Russian and English editions were published in New York in 1970. Soviet citizens publishing abroad had been flirting with criminal charges since the twenties: from 1929 to the early sixties few risked it. The cases of Brodsky, Sinyavsky, Daniel and Solzhenitsyn offered little comfort. Given all the changes in the political atmosphere, no one could predict how the authorities might react. On the one hand they probably wouldn't throw an old lady in the Lubyanka. On the other hand they might easily deprive her of her pension, her apartment, or anything else. They could easily ship her out of Moscow to exile in any of the distant places she so feared and loathed. Luckily, detente helped to make the 1970s the safest period for writers to publish abroad, and not until the end of 1979 did it become dangerous again.

That N. M. published her books abroad despite her fear shows the degree of her valor. She warned everyone, from Joseph Brodsky in the sixties to Christine Rydel in the late seventies. We received the same advice: don't come by taxi, don't call from a hotel, don't speak English as you approach or go away from the apartment, walk fast and don't do anything to make it conspicuous you are a foreigner, etc. When we arrived, she almost always closed the curtains in both rooms. When we said that the authorities weren't likely to do anything to an old woman, she just laughed—we were poor naive foreigners. "They" would do anything they pleased, and in the final analysis celebrity was no defense—"they" cared not a fig for public opinion.

I asked Joseph Brodsky last July [1983, E.P.] if N. M. had always been afraid, and he said, "When Marina and I first visited, she took fright, she didn't know who we were." But she seemed so extraordinary, so independent, it was hard to believe her fear. Here was a woman who was capable of saying *anything* about anyone and not giving a hoot about what people thought. But during our very first visit when Ellendea half-jokingly during an argument referred to something Marx had said as "stupid," N. M. turned pale and whispered to her, "Shh, don't ever say things like that here!" We visited her almost once a year for ten years, and her last words would always be a variant of "Well, next year I won't be here." Ellendea saw her for the last time in 1980 (I was denied a visa) and remembers the shuffling footsteps of N. M. coming to the door in pain, unlocking a whole series of locks. "She's still afraid . . . The woman is eighty years old and she's still afraid," Ellendea told me sadly.

Among N. M.'s specific fears was one that we found paradoxical, although she was not the only intellectual who expressed it. She was afraid of the *people,* the *narod.* The first time she said this, I asked her what she meant. She just pushed the curtain open, pointed outside and said, "There, them." She meant the ordinary people of Russia. All she had suffered through made her think that given the right signal, the bloodlust of the people could be turned loose again, and any passerby might be capable of destroying her and those like her—Jewish and intellectual. "They hate us," she said, "for what we have." If it weren't for the government, she said, they would gladly kill her kind. She admitted it was ironic that in this case the government was the protector of the intelligentsia. But the lower classes had immeasurably less than the "rich" intellectuals, and therefore they hated them.

N. M., incidentally, was extraordinarily afraid of *young* people, especially young Russians. She repeatedly warned us to be careful about whom we sent to her or brought to her. That is why in February of 1977 I was surprised that when during a private visit we explained we were

21

travelling with three young editors who worked at Ardis, she invited us to bring them with us. Normally, she would have objected. Ellendea had always wanted to introduce N. M. to her best Moscow friend, Tanya, but N. M. very unwillingly met her, and even in 1980 when Ellendea took her a second time, N. M. was very careful around her. Some of her suspiciousness doubtlessly came from her years of teaching English to the young. She hated teaching, and her experience was that young people were often likely to be informers.

N. M.'s books show her other side, the victorious side. I cannot imagine any other Russian with the courage to write, as she does in *Hope Against Hope*, "We all took the easy way out by keeping silent in the hope that not we but our neighbor would be killed. It is even difficult to tell which among us were accomplices to murder, and which were just saving their skins by silence." Even Solzhenitsyn lacked the courage to write that; he followed the Dostoevsky line that suffering precedes grace, and the Russians would save the "West" from Communism.

Both Mandelstams illustrated the truism that the quiet and meek person occasionally finds himself committing some act of singular bravery, which he himself cannot explain afterwards. Osip Mandelstam's attack on the Chekist Blyum is the most famous example. There was one in N. M.'s life too, and I don't think it has been written about. She describes it on a tape which Clarence Brown made in March 1966. In 1930, thanks to Bukharin, Mandelstam and she were spending two months in, of all places, a Central Committee sanitorium in the South. It was there that they got the news of Mayakovsky's suicide. Also living there, quietly, was the soon-to-be famous Commissar Yezhov. Though he had a limp, Yezhov liked to dance; he seemed to be a bit of an exhibitionist. That evening N. M. overheard one Georgian talking to another, saying that if a great Georgian poet had died, no Georgian People's Commissar would be dancing. N. M. went up to Yezhov and told him precisely what she had just overheard. "And the dances were immediately stopped," she said. There's a brief pause on the tape. And she adds the comment, "Not bad? I am like that, by the way." ("Nichego? Eto u menia est', mezhdu prochim.") This interrogative declaratory "not bad" ("nichego?") or "pretty strong stuff, huh?" ("sil'no?") was something N. M. characteristically put at the end of some especially amazing story.

Another interesting side to N. M.—which it is not customary to write about when recalling great Russian writers—was her attitude to sex. Given her own memoiristic practice and her insistence on saying everything fearlessly, it would be insulting not to record what she said. N. M.'s candor was all the more unusual since most Russians—especially women—are very puritanical when *discussing* sex and dishonestly reticent when writing about it. But for N. M. racy language was natural—and not just risque but very funny. The incongruity helped, of course, but I can't think of anyone who could make me laugh more with an aphoristic "obscenity."

She herself had never been pretty but had no doubt been pretty sexy. At least when we first met her one could still see signs of sex appeal. It was in her eyes and smile, her overall candor and charm, not in her body, which had probably always been very thin. From Blok to herself, anyone's peccadilloes could be the subject of a joke or information given in a spirit of fun and pleasure. I don't believe she ever condemned anyone (except O. M.) for anything. She said "indecencies don't exist" (*neprilichnostei net*). She told us how O. M. and she went to bed the first night they met, and speaking of Ellendea's beloved "roaring twenties," she dismissively said, "we invented all that." Again it was the free-spirited bohemian talking. She put up with almost everything from O. M., but, as she writes, when he got involved with Olga Vaksel, he made her very angry. She told Ellendea the story before we read the book. On tape she says it's the only time things got to the stage of divorce. Raya Orlova recalls being utterly stunned when N. M. took her into the kitchen and asked her if she knew the meaning of *ménage à trois*. Raya didn't. N. M. said the three of them lived together for six weeks and it was the most shameful memory of her life.

"Threesomes" came up several times in our literary discussions. One famous case—that of Mayakovsky, Lily and Osip Brik—she dismissed out of hand, since it appears that they all lived chastely in separate rooms. Explaining the background of Akhmatova's *A Poem without a Hero,* she said Akhmatova, Olga Sudeikina and Blok made love together. One of the letters N. M. wrote us in English gives some idea of the way she normally spoke of writers and literary heroes:

[1971]

Dear Ellendea and Karl!

I shall try to answer your questions on the "Poema bez geroia [*Poem without a Hero*]." First of all—it really happened that Olga spent a night with Blok. I think that "bez litsa i nazvan'ia" is not a quotation though it may be. I doubt that "Ia poslal tebe chernuiu rozu v

23

bokale zolotogo kak nebo ai" (Blok) was addressed to Olga. The poem from which are taken these lines is "V restorane"—1910. Olga's affair is dated 1912/13 (I don't remember). Akhmatova gave these lines to make sure that Blok would be recognized. Kuzmin was in love with Knyazev. He could not have been in love with Olga, but she used to come to Kuzmin. Akhmatova was in love with Knyazev. I don't know any particulars. Only that Olga and Akhmatova shared many lovers (Lur'e and others). Gumilev had nothing to do with it. At that time they lived a separate life. ("Razve my ne vstretimsia vzgliadom" is addressed to Nedobrovo who was Akhmatova's first lover.) Why Sudeikina rejected him? [Knyazev] How can one say? Women don't have to do whatever they are asked to . . . They may choose, may they not? Olga was one who knew why she picked and chose. Simply Akhmatova thinks that in this case she preferred Blok. Why not? "I kak vrag ego znamenit." It's of course Blok.

Perhaps Knyazev was one of Kuzmin's boys (as Yurkun). I am not sure of it. Read "Forel' razbivaet led." There must be something about this drama. Maybe Olga didn't like this kind of boys (as Yurkun, Georgii Ivanov) who make a job of it . . . They have both women and men (Yurkun, Ivanov). I don't know whether Knyazev was one of them.

The occasional playfulness of tone was very typical of her when talking about sexual choices.

Several people said N. M. herself had lesbian relations after O. M., and when she spoke of such things regarding Akhmatova ("there were some girls"), she never condemned them. However, she never said anything about her own history in this area. Once when she was showing us photos, there was one of her at about twenty, and Ellendea said, "You look very sexy in this picture." *Eto tozhe bylo* ("There was that too"), she answered with a laugh. And in our discussion of O. M. and her, she said that she had been unfaithful to him only a few times. She added, not just as a joke: "but I should have been more often."

Once we were talking about books we might send her, and I somehow brought up the subject of pornography. Immediately she smiled and said in a mock-begging tone, "Oh, if only you could get me some pornography! I love pornography!" Later Ellendea brought her *Cosmopolitan* and discussed its typical essays. N. M. was very interested in this. From *Cosmopolitan* the subject of *The Hite Report* came up. Ellendea told her about the subjects covered in that survey (masturbation, sexual styles, lesbianism). "Really," she asked, "could you send me a copy?" So we did. Christine Rydel took one the next year (1978). As Christine describes it, she and her husband, Wayne Robart, presented various things. First there were different kinds of Twinings

24

Tea and three bars of fancy English soap with the embossed crown of the Queen's Silver Jubilee on them. "I'm in luxury," N. M. said, and she sat up in her bed even though she had been very sick for some time, and stretched out her arm to give one of the bars of soap to a woman who had been taking care of her and who was just leaving. Christine also gave her Agatha Christie and P. D. James, who N. M. doubted could be as good as Agatha Christie, though she would give her a chance. The last book Christine got out was *The Hite Report.* Christine reminded her of the talk with Ellendea. N. M. started laughing and said something to the effect that well, I can't do anything now, I'm so sick. But grinning widely, she assured her that she would start *The Hite Report* when they left—"it'll be comforting anyway." Not many eighty-year-old Russian women would react like this.

In other ways N. M. was typically Russian. After a few years she was much more than politely solicitous about our family. As I have said, when we first met she approved of the fact that we had both been divorced; she said a good marriage could only come after a divorce. When, at the end of our Russian stay in 1969, my three sons unexpectedly came to live with us, her letters were full of questions about our and their well-being. We took all of the boys to Russia with us twice, and our middle son, Chris, by himself later. Our short visits to her with them were like family holidays for her. She remembered the scene of the three little boys sitting on the floor in her bedroom playing cards "as if it were yesterday," she wrote in February 1973. As early as 1972 she asked if we couldn't add a little girl—a suggestion fulfilled only in 1978 with the birth of Arabella. In letters she asked repeatedly if she could be the boys' grandmother, urging us to come again as soon as we had the money and could bring the boys. She asked us to promise to visit her first and said, "I shan't let you leave the kitchen."

I think N. M.'s feelings of tenderness for our family were in part another result of her own unhappy experience. She didn't have children with O. M., and thank God they did not. Their lives were tortured enough without giving "them" an innocent child to work on too. I think she liked it that somewhere in the world there was a normal place where a normal couple could live and bring up four children (a Russian family in this era is *one* child only, exceptions are rare), doing everything in a normal way. Aside from Russian literature and the things we had in common, I think that's what we were for her. We provided one way for her to release her feelings of warmth and kindness. In a peculiar way, it was these purely personal ties which were the key to our relationship, not so much the literary interests we shared.

But N. M., as well as a friend and a fascinating personality, was our first great teacher, a role the widows of Russia often played. She said of her country, "we have no society," meaning unofficial people had no way of having a community, a community with, first of all, simple communications. It is true there was, and is, no means of mass communication among them, but during the 1965-79 period such evenings and afternoons as her own *did* form the true community of cultured Russia. This community was limited mainly to the two capitals, but it did exist. N. M.'s evenings, and those of many other people, including other widows of writers, were important sources of information, places for the exchange of opinions, the teaching of history. Akhmatova's comment that this was a "pre-Gutenberg" era was apt. With the doors to printing plants and copying machines locked tight, carbon paper was probably the most powerful weapon left to free-thinking Russians. After that, there was talk.

The widows of writers preserved that genuine Russian culture which was locked up, blotted out, censored, and unmentionable not only in the official press, but everywhere that the Party rules: libraries, colleges, universities, theaters and movie houses, conservatories, art institutes, the Union of Writers, publishing boards, and state-run television.

For example, a young person who wanted to study Mandelstam (or Akhmatova or Gumilev or Acmeism in general) could not do so in a university, officially. As I write this, no course or seminar devoted to Mandelstam has ever been offered at any Soviet institution of higher learning; it would be virtually impossible to write a dissertation on him. (Conceivable exceptions: selecting some negative approach, such as an attack on "modernism," or falsifying things totally and claiming that at some point Mandelstam had been a revolutionary. Or an Armenian might ignore *Pravda*'s attack on "A Journey to Armenia" and write about that.) In our era no Soviet professor would dare direct a Mandelstam dissertation openly. Moreover, just assembling a Mandelstam bibliography and his works would be a huge chore, indeed an impossible one. The only comprehensive edition of his works (three volumes then, now four) has been published in the West with the help of CIA money, and in Russia such renegade editions are kept in "special repositories" in a few large libraries. Only politically reliable senior people or Party apologists can get access to such pernicious books. As for historical works or monographs that would provide trustworthy factual background—such things are nonexistent.

So the prospective young Mandelstam scholar, a person willing to risk suspicion by his very interests, would probably seek out an older faculty member with a liberal reputation, who—after a careful process of deciding whether or not to trust him—might privately tutor him and provide the books and bibliography required to get a start. A second step might be an introduction to Nadezhda Yakovlevna Mandelstam, who in private meetings like the ones we had with her, would be the prime source; she knew the truth about the past and would tell it.

N. M. did not take on such scholars easily. She was especially mistrustful and afraid of young Russians. But she did help serious scholars from many countries. Among the notable results were the books of Clarence Brown and Jennifer Baines. Other scholars she scorned. In spite of N. M.'s derisive opinion of standard literary criticism, she wrote it herself, in the memoirs and *Mozart and Salieri.* She helped many Mandelstam scholars in every way imaginable, from stories to introductions. She thought a young English scholar who was visiting her at one point was very clever and told us so. About the modern schools of criticism she was invariably negative. She was quite prejudiced against one well-known Western scholar, citing his request for formal proof of exactly when O. M. and she were married as evidence of someone who knew nothing about O. M. and the USSR. And she despised all kinds of syllable counting. She had great affection for Clarence Brown, although she periodically had "fights" with him, and in the end she had the entire O. M. archive moved from Paris to Princeton. Her trust in Clarence was the main reason for her final choice. In a more general way she wanted the archive moved from Europe to America because she did not think Europe, especially France, would long remain safe from the Communists. She hoped that if the day ever came when O. M. could be printed and studied freely in Russia, the archive would return.

N. M.'s memory was one of the primary resources for anyone doing serious research not only on Mandelstam but on the whole period. If one were attempting to reconstruct the portions of the Silver Age omitted in Soviet books, people such as she were essential. Her private "tutorials" and her evening salons were quiet but formidable ways of passing on Russian culture. She was not alone; there were many other widows too—survivors ranging widely in education, intelligence, memory, and the kinds of resources at their disposal. For example, N. M. at this time had virtually no books or manuscripts— the small Mandelstam archive was already out of her house and would be removed from the USSR at the start of the 1970s. When we were involved in such "archive discussions" with other widows, we emphasized the need to send copies of everything abroad. As N. M. knew—and as the others should have—the state archives had been the cemetery for a great deal of important material, some of which had actually been destroyed. N. M. was the only person we heard of in the literary world who actually sent the *originals* out of the country.

Both Russian and non-Russian specialists made their way to N.M. and other widows as they were writing their essays and dissertations—either official ones in the case of foreign students or private ones in the case of most Soviet devotees. Again, there was precedent in the last century. When Nicholas I banned the study of philosophy in the universities, it simply moved into the private circles and famous salons of Stankevich, Panaeva and others. Consequently influential writers such as Pushkin, Herzen, or Turgenev got their real educations not in the Tsar's schools, but in the philosophical salons of the day. N. M.'s two humble rooms were a far cry from the aristocratic drawing-rooms of the previous age, but the intellectual power she had was all the more impressive.

In N. M.'s case, especially, it was her unanticipated role as the conscience of the nation which drew people to her and made her, in a very quiet way, a teacher—not only a witness to poetry, but a witness to the unprecedented madness that had overwhelmed Russia after the Revolution. Being near her was also a way of touching the living poet Mandelstam. Her evening salons saw many discussions on literary topics, but I expect it was most often her frankness about the psychology and implementation of the Terror which people came to hear about. No one else dared say the things about Russia that she did in her sardonic style, in that charming low voice.

And, indeed, when N. M.'s second book of memoirs came out and her condemnation of some of the "literary heroes" of the twenties and thirties got *too* frank, the very people who had greeted her first book with enthusiasm began to abandon her. For all too many Russians there is a limit to the truth. The passion for hagiography is part of the passion to preserve the past. And to see that it is beautiful, just, and tragic.

Unfortunately, in the twentieth century, literature has become a very big business in the USSR. The official corporation has its own traditions, including construction of a huge, dull mass of secondary literature to support every officially sanctioned figure: after all, if a writer has many articles, books and dissertations written about him, memoirs and bibliographies, symposia, etc., one begins to be convinced that he *must* be significant. Even if he has become a first-rate Party hack like Fedin or Leonov, this *must* be true. After all, everyone (Russians and foreigners) reasons, if even his variant drafts, his diaries, and if his *Collected Works* in eight volumes were printed in an edition of 100,000 copies and are no longer available in any store—he *must* be important. Thus many foreigners have been convinced by the Soviet corporation, from Ernest J. Simmons in the past to Klaus Mehnert in the present.

A parallel secondary literature exists unofficially. No sooner does one get christened as a writer in the "central press," than people start keeping one's letters, arranging archives, doing questionnaires, and in general building a database for future historians, a supply of raw material that will make what was kept about Pushkin or Gogol look superficial. The Writer is a Holy Figure, so one has to be properly deferential. The Higher Truth is thus served (or serviced). I am quite sure that it will take future historians two centuries to work through all the mountains of crap that have been saved in the last sixty years about hundreds of Soviet Russian writers, official or not. N. M., in contrast, was devoted to separating the truth from the falsehood about her era.

The 1920s were a special theme for N. M. She saw little good in this much-praised era. To *any* specialist in Russian literature visiting Moscow in the 1960s and 1970s, this was an unexpected and disturbing heresy. A whole generation of Slavists who dominated Russian studies in the 1950s and 1960s, and nearly all Russian emigres of the first two waves, looked back on the twenties as an exciting period of experimentation and relative freedom. They taught everyone in my generation that this was proved by such things as the New Economic Policy, the incessantly quoted Party Resolution on the Arts in 1925 (which did not quite establish total Party control over everything— that would come a bit later), and the low number of executions.

Of course, there are some reasons to see things this way: (1) censorship was sloppier; (2) there was more editorial freebooting and "private" publishing houses existed; (3) the Party, even through its surrogates, such as RAPP, did not try to control absolutely every word; (4) a few new important writers were published—Babel's career began, Olesha published *Envy* and Bulgakov *White Guard*, Zamyatin was still a force, the poems of Pasternak, Mayakovsky, and a few others appeared. To these proofs one can now answer confidently: (1) the censors destroyed many works and were much stricter than pre-revolutionary ones; (2), Bulgakov's novel, for example, was not published completely because the journal it was appearing in shut

29

down; (3) the Party controlled anything it wanted to control, well enough in the cases of Mandelstam and Akhmatova to remove them from print; (4) Babel persistently and successfully lied about when his writing career began—we have learned that it wasn't in 1916 and then in the twenties under Gorky's tutelage, but in 1913 and in a paper that the Bolsheviks shut down; Zamyatin's *We* and most of his best work had either been printed before the Revolution or had to be printed abroad (in 1929 he asked to be allowed to emigrate, as did Bulgakov); the twenties were so good to Mayakovsky that he celebrated the decade by committing suicide as soon as it ended.

Many writers were silenced. The Cheka took care of Gumilev with bullets and arrested others. Many more emigrated—some under duress—and the rest of their work was published only abroad. Thus, Nabokov, Tsvetaeva, Khodasevich, Bunin and many others were no longer considered part of Russian literature. Not only were they expunged from Soviet textbooks, they were shunned almost equally by Western scholars and literary historians. For example, until the 1980s neither Nabokov, nor Tsvetaeva, nor Khodasevich were dealt with in any English-language history of Russian literature.

Those who stayed behind endured threats, searches, arrest, blackmail, private denunciation to the secret police, and public denunciation in the press and open forums. And for many of the best, just getting published in the twenties was an exception rather than a rule. This was true for Mandelstam, Akhmatova, Bulgakov, and dozens of others. The catalogue of names and devices used against them would fill several volumes. So N. M. not only had a point—she had *the* point. The direction was already clear in 1926. And one had to be more than a cock-eyed optimist to see the hungry years of the twenties as a period of great artistic freedom and accomplishment.

So when our friend Gary Kern, then a young scholar, spent an afternoon with N. M. asking her about his beloved Serapion Brothers, she totally devastated him—dismissing the school and nearly all the work. She did like the early Zoshchenko, she told him, both as a man and as the inventor of that funny narrator who personified this era. But Zoshchenko had had a very brief "true" career. As for the rest of the Serapion Brothers—well, one could see what their works turned into, if they survived. Most of them became officially acceptable Soviet writers: fat Tikhonov with his chestful of medals; Kaverin, who produced nothing of note after his first works, but solid Soviet classics, self-censored, cut over the years to fit the mold; Slonimsky and Ivanov, both of whom had some difficulties, but who started giving what was demanded and ended up as honored Revolutionary writers—Ivanov travelling abroad and residing in a comfortable dacha next to Pasternak; Fedin did best of all (and lived in the most fear, in some respects): he became the head of the Union of Writers and the notorious board that rejected and blasted Pasternak for his *Doctor Zhivago.*

Why should N. M. have thought otherwise about this period? It was in the twenties that the Mandelstams became used to starvation and homelessness. In *Hope Against Hope* she describes this with incredible calm and power, overwhelming the reader.

In the first book N. M. was still restrained enough, and general enough, to gain the praise of her countrymen. When in the second book she wrote with full candor, even the liberals and dissidents, the very people who had suffered along with her, were horrified. And in a fairly short time, she went from being a literary lioness to being almost an outcast in literary Moscow. She had aroused great controversy, as we discovered whenever we tried to defend her—an act we could risk only because we were foreigners.

Russia has a distinguished tradition of autobiographical prose which goes back to the middle of the last century. Annenkov's *An Extraordinary Decade,* Herzen's *My Past and Thoughts,* Tolstoi's trilogy *Childhood, Boyhood, Youth,* Korolenko's *A History of My Contemporary,* Nabokov's *Other Shores* (the Russian version of *Speak, Memory*), and Osip Mandelstam's *The Noise of Time* are among the main works of this tradition. Nadezhda Mandelstam's literary memoirs were worthy of this tradition. *Hope Against Hope* was published in Russian in 1970 as *Memoirs,* and in English in 1970. *Hope Abandoned* came out in Russian in 1972 as *Second Book,* and in English in 1974. These books revealed that she was not only a "witness of poetry" (her words) and witness to history, but a great prose writer whose permanent place in Russian literature remains secure.

But in Moscow this view was challenged after the second book came out. Many of those who lauded the truth of her first book refused to visit or speak to her after the second. A variety of open letters against her circulated in *samizdat.* At Christmas of 1973, she showed us one from Kaverin and asked us to publish it, which we did. It would show the outside world the character of Russian intellectual life. Veniamin Kaverin is still a well-known "liberal" writer. This literary argument typified the growing disarray and disunity in what Western observers of the USSR call the liberal camp. Clashing personalities played some part here, but other essentially internal strains were more

31

disruptive. Angry quarrels arose at this time over different reactions to N. M.'s books—and also over detente, the moral problems posed by decisions to emigrate, the Yakir-Krasin affair, and so on.

There was little official reaction to N. M.'s books, nothing analogous to the attacks on Solzhenitsyn which had been so vicious since the latter part of 1969, and no sanctions had been taken against her—but the outcry among the literary intelligentsia of Moscow and Leningrad was loud and vehement. Not since the revelations of Dostoevsky's debaucheries and weaknesses by his long-time friend Strakhov had there been such a furor. Almost everyone seemed to have a friend, favorite, or relative whom they thought she had slandered— and for that matter, many of her "victims" themselves were still alive and kicking. The chorus of complaint began with the circulation of her memoirs in manuscript, intensified each time one was published abroad in Russian, and reached its peak with the publication of the translation of the second book, *Hope Abandoned.*

The battle greatly resembled a domestic squabble. The Russian world of writers and critics is rather small, centralized, often hereditary, and occasionally incestuous. For Russians there is nothing strange about three Chukovskys being writers, about sisters being married to writers, wives moving from one writer to another (including wives who are also writers), the children of one writer marrying those of others (and being critics or translators themselves). Furthermore, it is centralized in two "capital" cities (and Moscow's suburban getaway, Peredelkino); and within Moscow, for example, hundreds of writers live in the same complexes of cooperative apartment buildings reserved for them. We could never decide whether this extreme propinquity was going to complicate the future history of Russian literature or greatly simplify it, but it is a fact to keep in mind. In addition, virtually all important publishing houses, literary periodicals, institutes for the study of literature and training of writers, and the main branches of the Union of Soviet Writers are located in Moscow and Leningrad.

N. M.'s decision to speak her mind, to record her frank view of the past and its cast of characters, to say things which no one before had dared to say about the public and private lives of hundreds of well-known people, made her many enemies in these centers of power. Some angrily broke off all relations, others simply stayed away to avoid getting into a fight, and many abused her from afar. She was called a gossip, a liar, a slanderer, a malicious old hag.

"It's all lies!" the elderly critic Emma Gerstein told me

indignantly, referring to *Hope Abandoned* and the positive review I had given it. "All lies?" I asked. "You mean there is *nothing* true in it?" "It's *all* lies!" she repeated even more angrily. Because N. M. describes Emma Gerstein as a bourgeois bungler and coward, I could understand the woman's bitterness (which poured out for twenty minutes). I listened patiently, but was embarrassed. On a previous trip a strange thing connected to these two women had happened to me. Ellendea and I had been visiting N. M., and talking about literature. N. M. knew that we had several close friends who all lived in the writers' apartment buildings on Red Army Street (Krasnoarmeiskaya)—and that Emma Gerstein lived there. That's the only explanation I can think of for the non-sequitur N. M. made as we stood in her little front hall ready to leave: "And nevertheless Emma *did* burn the poem" (*I vse-taki, Emma sozhgla stikhi*). And we left. This referred to the episode in *Hope Abandoned* where Emma Gerstein is said to have played it safe by burning a manuscript. By sheer chance a few days later I was introduced to Emma Gerstein for the first time by a mutual friend, and left alone with her. Following an hour of scholarly Lermontov talk, I got up to leave, and standing in her hallway, she suddenly said, "And I *never* burned anyone's poems." This is as close as I have ever been to a parapsychological event.

Gerstein's furor was understandable. N. M. stated that if Gerstein ever wrote memoirs, they would be full of prevarication. (Gerstein did write her memoirs, part has been published by Ardis in *Russian Literature Triquarterly*—strictly to show that anyone who wishes may challenge N. M. if they are brave enough to publish abroad.)

Curiously, at the end of our visits in the seventies, N. M. wondered sincerely how Emma Gerstein was getting along. Gerstein's blanket condemnation and Kaverin's illogical, but vicious letter are typical of the reactions to N. M. at this time. Everywhere we went we were given examples of what various people considered slander in her books— usually of friends or relatives. "X is not mentally unbalanced," "Y was never an informer," "Z did not destroy Mandelstam's poem." We could not judge each case, but as we kept asking everyone about the individuals in question, all of the serious charges made by N. M. were confirmed by at least one or two other people. That is, in one house I would be told, "Y was never an informer—that's slander" and in the next house that "everyone knows that Y was an informer." Most amazing to me was the case of the respected scholar N. Khardzhiev. N. M. says he was crazy, and that when he edited the long-aborning Soviet edition of O. M.'s poems, his textology was a joke—he would cut and rearrange lines and stanzas at will. Ellendea and I were told everywhere that it was absolute slander to call him insane and that his reputation as a loving text specialist precluded anything like what N. M. described. Much to my amazement, the next time we returned to Moscow, when a meeting between me and Khardzhiev was arranged, the very people who had assured me of his normalcy one by one called me aside and whispered special instructions about meeting him. Unanimously they said things like "he's *very* strange, you know," "if you say the wrong things, he can get completely hysterical," and otherwise instructed me about the extraordinary caution I should show, even if something unpleasant happened. (As it turned out, I didn't need the instruction, but it's interesting that his universal reputation was precisely what N. M. had dared to write.)

Moreover, on our next trip we also met the wonderful Iviches, contemporaries of Mandelstam's, very old friends. Ivich, well into his nineties, talked of knowing Gumilev and seeing Blok—we were stunned by both his charming personality and his knowledge. Ivich's unique archive included O. M.'s autographs. He showed me the poem "Ballada o lune," which Khardzhiev included in the Soviet edition. But Ivich's Mandelstam autograph is *totally* different. He explained that Khardzhiev had come to see it and had cut it and rearranged it to suit his own whim, saying "It's better this way." Ivich said he could hardly believe what he had seen; Khardzhiev had such a good reputation as a textologist, and before Ivich's very eyes he rewrote Mandelstam! In short, every time we had been able to cross-check, it turned out N. M. *was* right. Still, one must assume that anyone's memory can be faulty, and malice was not unknown to N. M. But these contradictions put the outsider in an untenable position, especially with Russian friends who would end by saying that X had expiated his crimes by a kindness later on, and that Y was a pitiful case and one should not attack him, even if justly.

There are two points which I would like to make, however: (1) for the non-Russian reader the specific individuals and names are not especially meaningful. The larger picture and moral viewpoint of N. M. were and are much more important to us. (2) In most cases the objections to her book, if one examines them closely, turned out to be objections to *opinions,* not to facts. Moreover, they were objections to negative opinions which are frankly expressed in forceful language.

Russian literary people are not used to this—they usually prefer the hagiographic approach to the past and writers' biographies. Anyone who has tried to write a biography of a Soviet writer runs into this when he reaches primary sources such as friends, colleagues, and widows. There is little of the rough and tumble of Western memoirs and diaries; a Russian Anaïs Nin would cause cramps; Harry Truman's bluntness and language would be totally unacceptable. Everything is recorded on a very elevated intellectual plane. Art is mentally capitalized, sex does not exist. And unpleasant historical events are glossed over or not mentioned. Ilya Ehrenburg's voluminous memoirs offer a good example—they were important for what they did rediscover for the young Soviet reader, but the world he described bore as much relation to the real world as Disneyland does to New York. It is precisely this kind of compromising memoirs that many of the liberals who were attacking N. M. preferred—or, at least, were accustomed to. The optimism, positivism, and smiling good health of mediocre socialist realism has had its unconscious effect. And so quite apart from the moral questions, such critics are locked in by a literary convention, a connection which goes back a very long way in Russian history.

Therefore it was no surprise that N. M.'s picture of Anna Akhmatova shocked many of the great poet's admirers. To such enthusiasts it was impossible to allow a talented artist such normal human traits as querulousness, egotism, or pettiness—let alone the veiled suggestion that she was occasionally attracted to beautiful women. Why discuss such things, they said, forgetting that every memoir about Pushkin is scoured for the details which make his personality come alive. Russians are very willing to gossip about all these things—but writing it down is a different thing entirely. N. M.'s description of the woman does not in fact lessen (or attempt to lessen) Akhmatova's art. But the dominant Russian view is that a good book cannot be written by a bad person, and this has led to a conspiracy to deny human attributes to beloved writers.

So Nadezhda Mandelstam came along like a Patton at inspection, frazzling communal nerves. Naturally, the reaction was angry among victims, friends of victims, and those whose careers her view of Soviet literature would turn into a null set. Some gave vent to their spleen in letters. And at least two sets of memoirs were written in response to N. M.'s. One by a liberal writer, Lydia Chukovskaya, is a prolix and contentious record, justified by her long friendship with Akhmatova; another, by Gerstein, I have mentioned above. We can read these anti-memoirs, and where the authors catch N. M. in errors of fact we should be grateful; where their opinions of people and views of events differ—as they must—we can consider them and test them. That there are some corrections in the first category was inevitable, given the span of years which her books cover; but it is clear that the majority of objections remain in the realm of opinion, viewpoint, and interpretation—as were Kaverin's charges, to which we now turn, since his attack represented a majority view. I have already published a translation of his letter to N. M. of March 20, 1973, in *The New York Review of Books*.

Veniamin Kaverin (b. 1902) began his career as one of the Serapion Brothers. Trick plots, detective and adventure stories are typical of his early work; his fairly numerous later tales and novels are less experimental and are all considered acceptable socialist realism. In 1956 he helped to bring out a mildly liberal "thaw" anthology entitled *Literary Moscow*. He has generally been what Westerners would call a liberal. His career has been as long as it is undistinguished. In the first volume of her memoirs N. M. calls him a perfectly decent man, but in two places she does tell stories which may be interpreted as showing him in a rather negative light.

Since many readers will not know N. M.'s books or be able to recheck them point by point, I think it is essential to comment on some of Kaverin's main charges. When citing N. M., Kaverin makes minor alterations in wording (including omissions) and punctuation in several of the quotations, and more importantly, he takes others *completely* out of context—adding his own interpretative wording around the quotation. Kaverin's claim that the goal of N. M.'s book is to show that modern Russian literature has not existed except for Mandelstam, Akhmatova, and herself is ridiculous—and it would not occur to anyone outside the Moscow-Leningrad literary world to read the book this way. If it is demeaning to report their treatment of Mandelstam and herself—and other victims of Stalin's terror—she does indeed demean and shame some writers. She is also justly critical of many of their works.

"Who gave you the right to judge artists who gifted their country and the whole world with their brilliant works?" Kaverin asks. A bizarre but symptomatic question—to ask of someone whose husband was murdered, with the help of writers, and whose life, along with those of her closest friends, was turned into constant terror. But beyond this—hasn't every individual the right to judge? To publicly express an opinion? The attitudes which I described above are implicit here—if a writer "gifts" the world with brilliant works, one has no right to lower Art to worldly levels by showing him in a bad light. Later on Kaverin criticizes N. M. for not having a "literary education"—only in a society where so many writers and critics now go through official literary institutes could a respected writer make such a ludicrous demand for official certification. (As it happens, N. M. did have an advanced degree in philology.)

Kaverin provides a list of "talented writers and honorable men" which runs from Gorky to Meyerhold and is presented as if the talent and honor of all these men were great and unquestionable. However I have heard the honor of nearly every one seriously questioned at some time or another (beginning with Gorky, whose vicious hypocrisy is almost universally admitted), and of course their literary merits are subject to the widest disagreement. Most important is that N. M.'s treatment of these writers—both personally and as artists—differs markedly from one to the next, and she is by no means always as negative as Kaverin suggests.

Of greater interest to Kaverin was the case of Yury Tynyanov. Tynyanov was his close friend, and, moreover, Kaverin married Tynyanov's sister—so he was not a disinterested party. Tynyanov (1894-1943) is regarded by many Western Slavists as one of the best critics of the Soviet period. Many Soviet critics agree, but there are few outsiders who would claim that his prose *fiction* is of interest to anyone but Russians.

I have reread everything N. M. says about Tynyanov, including the whole chapter entitled "Literary Scholarship," and in only one instance do her comments on him have to do with his personal character. Elsewhere she simply discusses his ideas on literary development. There is no basis for Kaverin's charge that she is trying to make Tynyanov "the chief of all the hypocrites in our literature." She calls Tynyanov a good man, "among the best and purest" of her contemporaries, and obviously feels sympathy for him—while believing his critical ideas were sadly misguided.

I think there are many scholars who would agree with most of her critique of Tynyanov's theories, and with her observation that he was the "son of a rationalistic age" with its faith in systems. She does not pretend to cover all of his works, and the fact that she does not also find good things to say no doubt offends Kaverin's Soviet sense of convention and justice. In any case, there is at least room for doubt that Tynyanov marks a new stage in world literary criticism, and Kaverin's enraged charge that "sick rapture over self" dictated N. M.'s book stems from family feelings, not analysis of facts and possibilities. If one looks carefully at the one extensive passage which Kaverin attempts to tear apart, one sees that the *only* objective fact under question is the precise length of a corridor.

Nadezhda Mandelstam is not Mandelstam's widow, Kaverin asserts, but his shadow—and a shadow should know its place. I think that she had some idea of her real place—and Kaverin's. Her desire to have Kaverin's letter published is evidence of this. In any case the letter is a literary document belonging to a widespread Russian genre ("A's letter to B"), and it has circulated widely in Moscow. And because it makes no sense to misquote and distort an author to the author herself, I must conclude that Kaverin was aiming at a wider audience. Had N. M. kept her peace, eulogized the liberals' idols of the past, and smilingly offered platitudes about Mandelstam, her last years would have been rewarded by continuing crowds of visitors, including those who once pretended not to recognize her. She could have played the grand role of poet's widow in the accepted way. But she alone broke free—and I think that the feeling of relief and justice must have more than made up for attacks such as Kaverin's, which she had experienced all her life. And because she was free, her books will remain in Russian literature long after Kaverin's are forgotten.

In private conversation and in letters N. M.'s literary opinions were as categorical as her socio-political ones. The iconoclasm of many of her views is less breathtaking today than it was a decade ago, but her decrees and awards have lost none of their pungency. Since she had been the wife of a great Russian writer, literature and life were very close for her, and she was keenly attuned to the traditions that O. M. was following. This was true even in the tragic things. For example, when telling how O. M. invented an ailment that required examination in Moscow, in order to persuade the watchdogs guarding his Voronezh exile to give him travel permission, "just to get away and have freedom at least for a day," N. M. said this was "like Pushkin" exactly— fabricating a health excuse to get permission from the police to travel. Pushkin was special to her, and when I told her I had translated his critical prose, she turned serious and warned me that this was an especially "responsible task." Since she and O. M. hated translation in principle, this was an extraordinary comment.

As for twentieth-century writers, she was usually acerbic and witty in her opinions. Often it seemed that something O. M. once said had inclined her permanently in one direction or another. We had told her that Ellendea had come to do research on Bulgakov, so she probably pulled her punches a little here; moreover, the unquestioning help that

Elena Bulgakova gave N. M. (through Akhmatova) when O. M. was arrested played a role in setting her opinion. On March 3, 1970, she wrote to us in English, as usual:

> I can tell you but very little about Bulgakov. We had never met but in publishing houses or in the street. For a year we even lived in the same house [building]. Akhmatova was a great friend of his. There is even a poem written after his death ...We met in 1921 in Batumi. He was in rags (we as well). Whenever we met he stopped us and asked: Can one win a prize for a novel. I rather laughed at him but Mandelstam said that there was "something" in this man, which meant that he seemed talented. The last time we met in the writers' union (*Soiuz pisatelei* in 1938. He had to put off his skates (he had been skating in the yard). He had some rash words with the waitresses. When we approached he stopped quarreling and smiled at us. I don't approve of quarreling with waiters but Mandelstam said he might do whatever he liked as he had a clever face. He really seemed clever and talented but very nervous and a bit sorry (or sad). This is my impression.

N. M. goes on to say that O. M. and she had read Bulgakov's *White Guard,* which was responsible for the shutting down of the journal in which it appeared, and they were at one of the performances of the play made from the novel, *Days of the Turbins,* a great and successful scandal when it premiered in 1926 at the Moscow Art Theater. She gave no opinion of it, but added that, "It was the only time that we were in that theater." I imagine this remark relays the O. M. and N. M. verdict on Stanislavsky and the "classic" Russian stage. N. M. also said that her brothers and Paustovsky had gone to the same school as Bulgakov in Kiev, the First Gymnasium, but she did not remember much more. Bulgakov was not really discovered by most people inside or outside of Russia until the publication of his novel *The Master and Margarita* in 1966-67. It was like light in the dark for most readers, and we arrived in Moscow on the wave of its popularity; but N. M. did not like the book. She considered it blasphemous (Bulgakov retells the Gospel story of Christ and Pilate); and she said this even before her most religious phase began.

Of Bulgakov's widow, Elena Sergeevna, on the other hand, she had only good things to say. N. M. herself got on the phone to Elena Sergeevna, told her about Ellendea's research, warmly recommended us, and arranged the first meeting between us and Bulgakov's widow. This was one of the first times that we saw the importance of the "network of widows." She tried to assist Ellendea in her Bulgakov research in another way too; when we mentioned plans to go to Kiev, she got excited and said Viktor Nekrasov was not only an honest writer and wonderful man, he was an admirer of Bulgakov. She planned to call Nekrasov as soon as our plans were definite, but unfortunately we could not work the trip into our schedule, so we did not get to meet Nekrasov until 1981 when we were all in Los Angeles together.

Among other Soviet prose writers her qualified favorites seemed to be Zoshchenko and Platonov (the latter was just emerging from oblivion at the time of our first visit in 1969). But the *unpublished* works of Platonov were especially popular among the kind of people who would soon come to be called dissidents. N. M. had already read the *samizdat* copy of Platonov's *The Foundation Pit.* His grim vision of the not-so-brave new world, a vision unparalleled for pessimism even in Russia's literature, struck her as simple truth, quite without artistic exaggeration. N. M. also noted his unique style, a disorienting mixture of the words and grammar of high literary tradition with the misunderstood words and twisted grammar of the prose taught by the Bolshevik regime. She introduced us to the young scholar E. Ternovsky, who gave us a copy; we smuggled it out and published it for the first time in 1973. Platonov's ambiguous attitude to the new world was problematic (a curious part of him wanted to be a helpful engineer for the "new men"), but N. M. does praise him in *Hope Abandoned.*

Zoshchenko is a better-known case, since she wrote more about him. Her books convey her respect for Zoshchenko's prose and his personal bravery. But they also show regret. She noted "poor, innocent" Zoshchenko's "sordid" decline in the late twenties, much earlier than most people's. What Nadezhda really liked, and doesn't explain in either of her books, was the early Zoshchenko. She told us he was profoundly original, that the narrator he "invented" in the beginning stories was the true, new Soviet man, the uncultured vulgarian up from the mob. Zoshchenko had gotten his language and his interests exactly right, and while he could use that persona he did original things. But satirists and states are mutually destructive, as Zoshchenko discovered, and we know that in the short run pens are not really mightier than swords.

The same was true for the playwright Nikolai Erdman, for whom N. M. had only praise. She said that she always delighted in the funny stories he *whispered* to her whenever they visited. He was a great wit, but he, too, was permanently terrorized; at the very end of his life he feared nothing more than ending up in *samizdat.* While *The Mandate* was performed in the twenties and *The Suicide* was rehearsed until

Stalin pronounced it dangerous, neither of Erdman's plays was ever published in the USSR. But then in the early 1970s manuscripts started circulating, and though he trembled, Erdman even had premieres in Germany and Sweden. It was because of N. M.'s enthusiasm that we eventually published the two plays together in English (1975), and we issued the first edition of *The Suicide* in Russian, with quotations from N. M. and Stalin together on the cover. It was intensely enjoyable to send her this book, but I don't remember what her reaction was. However, I do know that the fact that enthusiastic American audiences saw the play on Broadway is ultimately due to N. M.'s talks with us a decade before. Dostoevsky's Father Zosima was correct about light. N. M. shed the light—and it grew larger independent of her will.

Her opinions of poets were more complicated, naturally. But there, too, she had surprises. While on the surface one should imagine O. M. and Mayakovsky as implacable opponents, she dismissed Mayakovsky's theories, politics, and his Party-oriented LEF milieu (not to mention the connection to the secret police through Osip Brik's notorious salon), and said that Mayakovsky was simply "a nice fellow" (*milyi chelovek,* more precisely in her pronunciation, *milyi chik*).

Pasternak, on the other hand, who on the surface would seem to be like O. M., was a very complex case for her. *Hope Abandoned* provides a fairly detailed "balance sheet." There had been friendly times; she recalled "madly curious" O. M., Pasternak, and herself walking the crowded streets together right after Lenin's death. When we knew her, she still had warm and frequent relations with some members of his family. But there were definitely episodes from the past that still rankled. In the first place, it was not common for Russians to love both Pasternak and Mandelstam equally. One was often asked to pick one or the other (in the nineteenth century the choice was Tolstoi or Dostoevsky). The question "whose poet is yours?" is a vital one.

More important for N. M. was the celebrated episode of Stalin's phone call to Pasternak, not completely forgiven. When O. M. was arrested, Bukharin wrote a letter of defense to Stalin; and this letter apparently ended with the phrase, "and Pasternak too is very worried," it being known that since Pasternak was the translator of Stalin's Georgian poetry, there was a more than casual personal connection. N. M. assumed, as did others, that Bukharin's letter explained Stalin's personal call to Pasternak in May 1934, when he asked if O. M. was a "genius." However, Pasternak did not tell N. M. or other immediate principals about this call or its apparent purpose. Indeed, months passed before a friend learned of the call and brought it to N. M.'s attention. She said that she had "big conversations" with Pasternak on this account. A scrupulous and detailed account appears in *Hope Against Hope,* but my impression is that N. M. was not completely satisfied by Pasternak's explanation.

Pasternak's cautious attitude to the fate of a fellow poet seems fairly consistent to me. He had a perfect chance to warn Marina Tsvetaeva not to return to Russia when he talked to her in Paris in 1935; but he did not make the effort to persuade her of the obvious. He failed to tell what he knew—and she ended up on a rope. Such things as this, and Pasternak's ambiguous but basically pro-Stalin stance until 1937, probably account for N. M.'s continuing hostility to Pasternak. It took various forms. For example, though she knew it existed, and though she had access to it, she did not provide us or other scholars with the New Year's laudatory letter from O. M. to Pasternak. When we were given the letter by other hands and published it in *RLT,* we thought that N. M. might not forgive us for failing to hold her fort. But she said nothing about it.

Her ambivalent feelings toward Anna Akhmatova are now well-known, particularly since much of the polemic over *Hope Abandoned* stemmed from the unvarnished portrait of Akhmatova discussed earlier. (Supposedly the scholar Koma Ivanov persuaded N. M. to delete the open references to lesbianism and Akhmatova from the text of her book.) To us, however, it was absolutely clear that N. M. both loved and respected Anna Akhmatova. But the element of competition was still there, since Mandelstam and Akhmatova were intimate in a way which shut out N. M. at times.

Akhmatova and N. M. were very close in many ways—they had shared so many things in their long lives, and it was clear that it was a very deep friendship. But N. M.'s role was that of listener and Akhmatova was the star. Certainly there were tensions. For example, Brodsky says that he first knew about N. M.'s book in 1967 but that Akhmatova apparently had not yet even heard of it. Since it was begun in 1964, Akhmatova was clearly not a first reader.

As is often true, it was one thing for N. M. to criticize Akhmatova, another for someone outside the circle to do so. N. M. would quickly come to Akhmatova's defense if anyone attacked her unjustly or ignored the way Russia had treated one of its greatest poets. When the BBC did a dispatch on the death of Akhmatova, N. M. was extremely angry at their claim that Akhmatova's death had made a great impression in Russia. This was absolutely false, N. M. said, and it was very insulting that such a lie should be told. In fact, only a small group of admirers really knew what Akhmatova meant to Russia: for the official world she was Zhdanov's carrion, and to the masses of people she was unknown after a lifetime of repression.

When I was translating Akhmatova's *A Poem without a Hero,* N. M. was extremely helpful; she wrote fascinating letters, providing background material which I included in the notes (without being able to name her specifically). As N. M. herself observed in a letter, she had concealed her honest opinion of the work because she preferred not to be negative about a friend. Thus on April 1, 1971 she wrote: "Some words about the poem. I don't like it so I have very little to say." She mentions, however, that the third dedication was to Sir Isaiah Berlin, who was also the "guest from the future," and explained many of the mysteries of the poem. "Don't look for any double sense in *The Poem*—only one: the suicide of a boy with whom Akhmatova was in love. She had the feeling that she didn't save him." After all of this useful information, on November 25, 1971, she wrote again and said she really couldn't tell us much about the poem!

> There isn't any other idea that isn't clear from the first sight. But the poem is a bit mysterious. It is sheer coquetry from the part of the author: *"u shkatula dvoinoe (troinoe?) dno"* [the box has a double (triple?) bottom]. (Don't give it as my opinion! She was my friend and I don't want to give my opinion on her verse!) This coquetry is a compensation for the lack of ideas. She was in love with the man who had committed suicide. She hated the poet who had sent a black rose and she loved the woman for the love of whom the suicide was committed. Her idea is that the "desyatye gody" [the 1910s] in literature were not a "serebryanyi vek" [Silver Age] but a very perverse and dangerous period. Was the poet who sent the black rose responsible for the suicide of the boy? Even the woman was not...He was one of Kuzmin's set...As well as Olga (the heroine). She was a "nevinnyi tsvetok teatral'nykh uchilishch" [an innocent flower of the theater schools]. Kuzmin loved them in his way. I don't love the poem though there are beautiful parts ("i ves' traurnyi gorod plyl").

She really thought Akhmatova was guilty of false significance in this work. In another letter she concluded, "I don't like the poem. Things like *'lishniaia ten''* [extraneous shadow]—mean nothing but are intended to make the poem *'tainstvennyi'* [mysterious], which is not making it better." But she knew opinions in letters were quite different from dicta in printed memoirs, where her views are softened.

43

As for contemporary writers, especially poets, N. M. did not claim to have anything but hastily formed opinions, again at least partly based on the civic position of the writer. In the case of the four best-known poets, three official and one a "parasite" (according to the government charges against him), her judgments followed those of the majority of the people we knew. Yevtushenko and Voznesensky, said this general view, were both overrated, cynical tools of the regime; and their reputation in Western circles for being liberals or even dissidents was ridiculous.

Bella Akhmadulina, on the other hand, who had been Yevtushenko's wife, N. M. pronounced a "wonderful chick" (*chudnaia baba*), partly because of the poetry and partly because she had heard the same anecdote which we heard everywhere in 1969. As the story went, Akhmadulina was visiting Georgia, that warm republic with a reputation for hospitality and wine, and the birthplace of Stalin. And while his statues were gone everywhere else, a few were left in Georgia, where Stalin was still considered a great man, one of their own. So when at a large banquet the usual rounds of extravagant toasts were made, and a Georgian made a traditional toast to the "great Stalin," Bella, already fairly high, took off first one shoe and threw it at him, and then the other, and walked out barefoot. Partly because of N. M.'s warm words about her, the only public poetry reading we ever attended in Russia was by Bella Akhmadulina.

N. M.'s relations with Joseph Brodsky were complicated to say the least. He already had a unique reputation among the Russian intelligentsia, and was regarded as the best poet (not only the best, but out of competition). It was not surprising to hear Bella Akhmadulina say this; but even respected poets of the older generation such as David Samoilov agreed.

Apparently N. M. first met Joseph in either 1962 or 1963 when he came with Anatoly Naiman and Marina Basmanova to visit her in Pskov, where she had been teaching. Joseph first read her memoirs in 1968-69, or at about the time we met her. When he returned from exile, he became one of her visitors when he happened to be in Moscow. Brodsky was then known as one of "Akhmatova's boys," a group of young poets that also included Naiman, Evgeny Rein, and Dmitry Bobyshev (all shown in a memorable photograph taken at Akhmatova's funeral).

At this time N. M., like others, was slightly ironic about Akhmatova's boys, mainly because Akhmatova had a rather queenly air, and took it as a given that she was a great and suffering poet due all

the respect they and others gave her. But Joseph recited his poetry at
N. M.'s and she read his poems regularly. She thought he was a genuine
poet. But her attitude was always that of an older, and somewhat
worried, critic. She was not a mentor, but she was a link with O. M. and
the real past of Russian poetry, so she had some claim to such
judgments. She said, at various times, that he had some really fine
poems, and some really bad ones. As usual, she was skeptical about any
long forms, one of Joseph's special talents. She claimed that he had
"too many Yiddishisms" ("ivritismy") in his poetry, and said that he
had to be careful, that he was getting sloppy. It was honest worry about
the "pupil." Perhaps his personal behavior played a role too, I don't
know. When she first told Ellendea and me about him in the spring of
1969, we knew very little about him. She laughed and said that when he
called her up and said that he was in town and would be over in two
hours, she took it with a grain of salt. He might start drinking with
friends and show up much later, or she might as well go to bed, because
he wouldn't come at all. Nevertheless, she thought it was quite
important that we should meet him when we went to Leningrad, and
she provided a note of introduction. This turned out to be quite fateful
in our lives.

A peculiar call came from her just before we left for Leningrad.
She warned us that when we went to Leningrad we should not meet or
have anything to do with a man named Slavinsky, who was known as a
drug user. Later we found out that she had reason to worry: another
American was picked up by the KGB because of his connection to this
man's circle.

N. M.'s opinion of Brodsky grew harsher with the years, and in
Hope Abandoned she is more severe than in her first book. She mixes
praise and reserve: "Of all the younger friends who made life easier to
bear in her [Akhmatova's] last years, he was the most serious, honest
and selfless in his relations with her. I think Akhmatova overestimated
him as a poet—she was terribly anxious that the thread of the tradition
she represented should not be broken." After describing his
remarkable reading as being like a "wind orchestra," she says: "He is,
nevertheless, a remarkable young man who will come to a bad end, I
fear. Whether a good poet or not, the fact is that he is one, and this
cannot be denied him. In our times it is hard luck to be a poet—and a
Jew into the bargain." Later in the book, apropos of the selfless deeds of
Frida Vigdorova (who transcribed Brodsky's trial—a bold journalistic
first in the USSR), she says, "Brodsky has no idea how lucky he is. A
spoiled darling of fate, he fails to appreciate it and sometimes mopes. It

is time he understood that a man who walks the streets, the key to his own door in his pocket, has been well and truly let at liberty." She wrote us a letter on "February 31," 1973, after Joseph left Russia, saying "Give my love to Brodsky and tell him not to be an idiot. Does he want to feed the moth once more? We have no mosquitoes for such as he because he deserves only the North of our country. So let him be happy where he is, he aught [sic] to be it. And he will learn the language which he had longed for all his life. Did he master English? If not, he is crazy."

Joseph, incidentally, unlike many, praised N. M.'s second volume of memoirs very highly, in spite of what she said about him and in spite of the controversial portrait of Akhmatova. We wrote N. M. and told her Joseph's opinion. A month later Hedrick Smith replied (February 3, 1973), and asked us to "tell Josef that Nadezhda ... was delighted to hear about him and to receive his 'deep bow'. Nad. of course was flattered to hear his praise of the 2nd tome." Indeed, Joseph repeatedly defended N. M.'s right to say what she thought; he told Lydia Chukovskaya that if she was upset (she was), the simple thing to do was write her own memoirs in reply (she did).

What N. M. considered Joseph's unreliable behavior (not typical at all of the years when we knew him) bothered her, but even when joking, I think, her attitude showed a warm affection for him. In 1976 Joseph had a triple by-pass operation which terrified all of us. Soon after we went to Moscow, and visited Nadezhda as usual (February 15, 1977). When I told her that Joseph had had a heart attack, without thinking for an instant and with her usual smile, she said, "Fucked himself out?" ("Pereebalsia"?) She always inquired about him and always asked us to say hello. During the years of her efforts to get the O. M. archive moved from Paris to America, she repeatedly asked us to relay messages to Joseph, whom she regarded as one who would honorably see that this most important request was carried out.

N. M.'s disagreements with Joseph had gone on for many years, before we knew either of them. The main literary quarrel which they had seems to have been over Vladimir Nabokov. Bear in mind that in these years Nabokov was forbidden in the USSR, that his early Russian books were all extreme rarities, seen by no one but book collectors of the highest caliber. A Russian might chance to get an English novel by Nabokov, but not an original Russian one. (I knew two collectors who had copies of Nabokov's first real book, a volume of poetry published in Russia before the Revolution, but they were exceptions.) The only way a Soviet was likely to know much about Nabokov was from an occasional Chekhov Publishing House book, notably *The Gift (Dar,* 1952), reprints of the Russian *Invitation to a Beheading* and *The Defense*, done like many other Russian classics with money from the CIA. And when Nabokov translated *Lolita* into Russian in 1967, books were printed again with a subsidy from the CIA and these volumes circulated fairly widely in liberal circles.

N. M. had read *The Gift,* and that was the only work she accepted. Joseph and she had a major blow-up over Nabokov. Joseph insisted he was a great writer—he had also read *The Gift* as well as *Lolita, The Defense,* and *Invitation to a Beheading.* He praised Nabokov for dealing with the "vulgarity of the age" and for being "merciless." In 1969 he insisted that Nabokov knew the "masshtab" (values, true scale) of things, and his place in that scale, as any great writer must. He told us around 1970 that of the prose writers of the past the only two who meant anything to him were Nabokov, and more recently, Platonov. N. M. disagreed vociferously; they fought and did not see each other for quite a while (the quarrel lasted two years, he said). She never gave us her version because she knew I was a Nabokov scholar and that we had met the Nabokovs in 1969. She didn't say to me as she did to Joseph and Golyshev that in *Lolita* Nabokov was a "moral sonofabitch." But she did argue the first time we met her that one thing she had against him was "coldness" (a frequent Russian charge), and she said that in her mind there was no doubt that the man who wrote *Lolita* could not have done so unless he had in his soul those same disgraceful feelings for little girls (another typically Russian attitude, that reality always lies just under the surface of fiction). We could have pointed out that this was a curious underevaluation of imagination for someone who understood poetry so well. Instead, we took the easy way and argued on her grounds. We told her that nothing of the sort was true, explaining that Nabokov was the picture of respectability, and that he had been married to the same woman for thirty years and had dedicated every one of his books to her. She seemed disappointed. But obviously she was not yet convinced. A few months after we returned from Europe she wrote us a rather cranky—but typical—letter in which she said, first, that:

> I didn't like what [Arthur] Miller wrote about me. I am more interested in Scotch and detective stories than in such idiotic words. Did I say anything like that to you? Never! To him neither...I bet...[...] This pig of a Nabokov wrote a letter to the *New York Review of Books* barking at Robert Lowell for his translation of Mandelstam's verses. It

reminds me of our barking at each other about translations...A translation is always an interpretation (see your articles about Nabokov's translations, let alone *Eugene Onegin*). The publisher sent me Nabokov's article and asked me to write some words. I did at once and used very noble words in it which I avoid to do...In defence of Lowell of course.

Ellendea and I saw no reason to repeat this insult to Nabokov, and we were slightly embarrassed when he asked us to take her a copy of his Lowell article. The delicacy of our position was intensified by the Nabokovs' concern for N. M. We agreed that judicious silence, followed by a campaign to change her mind, was the best course, particularly in view of her fight with Brodsky on the one hand and the Nabokovs' generosity on the other.

Perhaps the most curious thing about the disagreement between N. M. and Brodsky over Nabokov is that in the course of the next decade they almost completely changed positions. Brodsky came to value Nabokov less and less, considered his poetry (which we published in 1976) beneath criticism and regarded him as much less significant. I would guess that part of this was a natural development, but Nabokov's dismissive critique of Joseph's *Gorbunov and Gorchakov* in 1972 hurt him very much. When Joseph finished the poem, he said, he just sat around for a long time, convinced he had performed a great feat. I agreed. I sent the poem to Nabokov, and then made the mistake of conveying his response, in softened form, to Joseph around New Year's 1973. Nabokov wrote that it lacked form, the grammar was faulty, the diction "kasha" and generally *Gorbunov and Gorchakov* was "sloppy." Joseph's face got dark, and he said "etogo net" ("there is none of that"). He told me about the fight with N. M. then, but after that I don't recall any good words from Joseph about Nabokov.

On the other hand, N. M. started changing her opinion of Nabokov rather rapidly, and by the mid-1970s she had only praise for him. When we asked what books she wanted, she always named Nabokov. For example, when I sent her a card and she actually received it through the open mail (she always said she rarely got things), she passed the word on through a Slavist saying she had received it July 12, just before leaving for two months in Tarusa. She asked him to request that we pass on "English or American poetry or 'something by Nabokov'." I remember that when I got out the presents for her during the 1977 Book Fair, the first item out of my bag was *The Gift* in our

Russian reprint. She was extremely happy, smiling a smile that would make any publisher's heart melt. I like to think that Ellendea and I played a role in this change; in the early days we were Nabokov's main Western propagandists in the Soviet Union, his true admirers and his Russian publishers as well. (I got the advance copy of *Ada* in Moscow in 1969, and Ellendea and I fought over who would read it first. When we were done, we lent it to our Russian friends.) We also had relayed to N. M. the Nabokovs' kind words about her husband. The last few times we saw her she always asked us to pass her greeting to Nabokov and praised his novels. When Ellendea saw her for the last time, on May 25, 1980, N. M. asked her to tell Vera Nabokov that Nabokov is a "great" (*velikii*) writer, and that when she had said bad things in the past, it was exclusively out of envy. She did not know that as early as 1972, Vera Nabokov had sent us money, asking that we use it discreetly to buy clothes for Nadezhda Mandelstam or others whose situation we had described to the Nabokovs during our first meeting with them in 1969.

While we knew a great deal about her life in literature, we did not know a lot about N. M.'s everyday life, so I cannot even attempt to describe it during the period of our friendship. Our contacts were special, our visits were exciting interludes. We wrote to her whenever a letter could be hand-delivered, we sent postcards when we travelled on vacations, and a few times we even called her. Around March 1, 1978, we got an urge and telephoned her. She sounded fine and said that she was studying Spanish, "just to keep my mind busy!"

One decision which was extremely important in her life, and which we do know something about, was her decision to emigrate. Like many others, when the possibility of leaving the Soviet Union became real in the early 1970s, she wavered. Indeed, she vacillated in such a way, and for so long, that we sometimes doubted she was being serious and thought it was some kind of mind-game she could not resist. But the sheer chance of leaving forced everyone who was even partly Jewish to consider the possibility. Of course great moral battles were fought over the ethics of leaving the motherland.

We do not know all of her considerations, but they had to include such things as leaving the land where Mandelstam was buried (even if no one knew where), leaving old friends, leaving the care of people who were her admirers, wondering whether she could survive an old age in a foreign place without close friends, being able to live on her royalties from the Swiss bank, and so on. She wrote to us on August 14, 1972, and said: "I returned home two days ago (I was on a visit to Pskov) and found your letter. I was touched that you think about me. I shall decide about my application in September. It is too hot now to move." But apparently the vacillation went on for two more years, until 1974.

Joseph Brodsky had last seen her during his seventy-two hours in Moscow before leaving Russia forever and meeting me in Vienna on June 5, 1972. Joseph and Victoria Schweitzer recollect that N. M.'s would-be emigration involved her old friend, Natalia Ivanovna Stolyarova. Stolyarova had been Ehrenburg's secretary; she had been in prison until 1949, and in the 1960s she had travelled in the West. It was natural for her to be a frequent guest at N. M.'s apartment and to tell her what impressions she had of the West. N. M.'s "final" decision involved her friends, the Khenkins, who were going. One version is that she decided to leave to go with them; the opposite version is that later she said, "they were trying to get to Europe using me." In any case she did apply to OVIR (Office of Visas and Registration) for an exit visa in 1974. The chronology is not clear, but the Khenkins were turned down, while she was *not*. Stolyarova then went to OVIR and withdrew N. M.'s application. One version holds that Stolyarova did this on her own, and even said she was clever to do so, because N. M. would have had to be all alone. The more reliable version is that Stolyarova persuaded N. M. that she was making a serious mistake and that N. M. asked her to retrieve the papers. Given N. M.'s strong will, I think the latter is more likely.

Whatever the exact truth of this episode, Ellendea and I can bear witness to the significant thing: for a period of time N. M. was very serious about leaving Russia and going to the West. She wrote to us about it. We kept hearing rumors one way and then the other. When we saw her, she confirmed the vacillation, mentioning factors such as those I listed above. We hesitated to give advice, since the results might turn out to be good or bad; we just gave her as much information as possible. We discouraged most people who asked about emigrating because they seldom foresaw all the consequences that would follow— especially if they were old. Even those who thought they knew all about the United States or England in fact had no conception of the realities of employment, housing, etc., not to mention culture shock. Our line was that they must really and truly hate their lives before they should consider leaving.

In N. M.'s case there was a special consideration. She was

adamantly negative about the "third wave" of emigration. One day she told us that the first wave (from around 1917) was comprised of the flower of Russian culture, the best Russian minds, the true aristocracy and intelligentsia. The second wave (after World War II) was already much worse—it was just "nothing." As for the new, third wave of the 1970s, she said, quite viciously, it was made up of "dregs, simply dregs" (*podonki, prosto podonki*). She delivered this dictate early in the emigration, before it included so many writers and artists, but given her mind-set, I'm not sure that even later she would have seen much difference between these ex-Soviet writers of note and the hustlers from Odessa.

Of course, there was nothing Jewish about her culturally, even though she could speak of "us Jews always being persecuted." Her tendency was toward the Russian Orthodox Church and she appeared to be ignorant of the basic texts of Judaism. (This was true of many of our friends from the intelligentsia.) However, I should note that she had strong pro-Israeli feelings, which I think were much more political than religious. And she did tell us it would be wonderful to see Jerusalem, although she doubted she would ever manage to. (This is still ambiguous, since it is not just a Jewish city.) As she grew older, her Christianity became stronger and more important.

N. M. gave us her Russian world, and we had nothing to give in return but our love and respect. We could only give her small gifts, but sometimes they were important to her comfort. What did a seventy-year-old Russian woman, the famous widow of a famous poet and the author of some of the most unprecedented and intrepid memoirs ever written, need in the 1970s?

She was so poor that it would have been hard to choose a bad present, but we soon learned her priorities. Over the years we did not often take N. M. gifts of clothing since she had little interest in such things. N. M. liked to insist that she was "not a woman any more, just a person." We resisted this definition—both from instinct and because of empirical observation. N. M. was endlessly interested in what Ellendea wore. It is true that Ellendea and I intentionally dressed the way we did normally. At first this was instinct but then we saw that most Russians preferred this to the common foreign students' attempt to dress like natives and melt into the crowd. When they had a real live American on their hands, Russians wanted him at least to look like an American. So N. M. was always studying Ellendea's outfits with great sensual pleasure, especially examining boots and belts. She would feel the fabrics with delight, and once touched a heavy belt made of brass disks linked by chains that Ellendea wore, saying *"kakaia prekrasnaia shtuka"* (what a fine item!).

On one early trip Ellendea took N. M. an Italian poncho. She needed help getting it on right the first time but loved it in a very female way, and wrote us later: "The poncho makes me warm and cozy. My friends simply rave about it. They have never seen such a fine thing. I adore it. And the towels as well" (January 27, 1971). Anyone who has ever used a Soviet towel will realize that fluffy American towels are a great luxury there, and such things were a sharp contrast to everything else in her apartment. While she could insist that all she wanted was books, that she was "just a person," Ellendea noticed that the perfume and soap which we took her were soon used up; over the years we interspersed the books and food with such useful things as designer sheets and bath oil sets. In the Soviet Union, in her world, they were little sensations. Sometimes there were specific requests. On Ellendea's last visit in 1980, N. M. was well enough to request things for herself and for friends—a wool dress and sweater in 3 sizes, one in blue for "a young lady."

In the early years, while she was still a hostess and had not yet been shunned, we and everyone we sent concentrated on the basics. Food and liquor—or vice versa. We would stock up at a Beriozka hard-currency shop or the special hard-currency grocery store on Dorogomilovsky Street, the haven of all hungry diplomats in Moscow. Whenever a good friend travelled to Moscow, we gave precise instructions on how to find this institution, the perfect example of Russia's callous treatment of her own people, since only foreigners and Russians with "certificates" could shop there. Anything we got there was fine, because N. M. always needed everything. Cheap, untaxed vodka, gin and whiskey were high on the list, because she had to entertain so many people; and for Russians bottles are the first priority. Then cigarettes, sugar, tea, cheese, butter, sausage, any canned goods, and so on—always basics, never anything like caviar (which at, say, the Briks', was obligatory). In her first letter to us in October 1969, N. M. lamented, "My whiskey supply has been done away with," and there was no one to renew it. When we got to know her well, we always added some rubles to keep her going, and Clarence Brown would send money from her Western royalties to change into rubles for her. I think a fair amount of royalty money reached her through various channels in the beginning. Joseph Brodsky recalls that when she got the special certificates for use in hard-currency stores, she was extremely generous with them and the wonders they bought. Russians, especially poor-looking Russians, were usually stopped at the doors by police, but Joseph brazened it out and went in to get American cigarettes.

But the best gift was a book. In this respect she was like most of the Russians we knew. It wasn't that "worldly" goods were scorned but book deprivation was more painful. Since we were so innocent and ignorant in 1969, this intense need made a special impression on us.

There may have been others, but the first book I remember giving N. M. was the Bible, and after that her own books, both in Russian and English. She liked all kinds of books and magazines in English. She often asked for English or American poetry; she was especially interested in T. S. Eliot in the early seventies, because she thought he and Mandelstam had some points in common. She asked us for Eliot's poems (I think she had read his essays), but later lost interest in him. When I gave her a copy of Kazantzakis's *Odyssey*, she measured its bulk, and said simply, "I don't believe in long forms of poetry." I think she suggested I give it to someone who would appreciate it.

By 1973 when we had already done so many reprints, she always wanted O. M.'s books, *Stone* and *Tristia*, and the three-volume Struve compilation of O. M. We supplied copies of these as often as possible— and she gave them away just as fast. (I don't ever recall seeing more than a few books in her apartment.) From Star Walter in the early seventies to Christine Rydel in 1978 we dispatched many brave friends; they were anxious to have the privilege of meeting her and helping her. Bear in mind that the bureaucrats in charge of the American exchange program for scholars and graduate students gave stern warnings about such activities, that most embassy people disapproved of exchangees meeting with "troublemakers," and that most American exchange students and professors refused to jeopardize their future ability to get visas by dealing with unapproved people, money or books. Indeed, after the name "Ardis" became known, American officials here and there warned Americans not to handle such dangerous things as Ardis books. We felt angry and ashamed when we heard this. On the other hand, we were proud that there were exceptions every year in each group, and they were given an opportunity to learn what the Russian intellectual experience truly was.

I do not want to give the impression that N. M. or any other "great-souled Russians" spent every day immersed in the classics. Her tastes were definitely not all highbrow. She loved Agatha Christie novels, which we sent repeatedly. In an early letter to us she wrote, "I've got three books by Agatha Christie from you and I thank you ever so much ... There's a writer!" (December 15, 1970). The next year she was more specific about why this kind of entertainment and relaxation was so valuable to her (it was unavailable in the USSR because the detective story was considered a "bourgeois mass market product" intended to keep the minds of the masses off serious social problems; now, however, they've begun to do their own version, with correct ideology): "I've a wonderful book of Agatha Christie about old women (ga-ga) and children. Thank you very much. For two days I forgot everything and lived in the realm of English little town gentry, clergymen, and so on ..." (October 21, 1971). Precisely this kind of escape and freedom is what Soviet readers lack. I think in a way N. M. found the same freedom and the same associations with another world in the Twinings tea she especially used to request—it wasn't that she really preferred the Twinings to the powerful brew that O. M. had taught her to make, it was the whole world of associations that made it taste good—a little whiff of a place where people did not live in fear, where the law was respected, where life was stable.

Sometime after 1975, as I have mentioned, she always added Nabokov to the list of books she wanted. But we also continued to send Mandelstam's books, notably the handsome edition of his *Voronezh Notebooks (Voronezhskie tetradi)* edited by N. M.'s friend V. Schweitzer. After we had published three hundred books I had become blasé about many things, but the evenings I spent typesetting these poems were very exciting. On the occasion of her birthday in 1979, we wanted to send her the *Voronezh Notebooks,* but the result was a typical Soviet story. Ellendea wrote a friend in the embassy a persuasive note, asking him to get a package to N. M.: "N. Ya's birthday is October 30—and this year is her 80th birthday. Ten years ago my husband and I met her for the first time, just at the time she achieved fame for her first book and was the old darling of the Moscow intelligentsia. When her second book appeared a few years later, many of the people who had hailed her as a genius and teller of truth in 1970 decided that she had washed too much linen in public, and they abandoned her. During recent years she has been increasingly shut-in due to poor health." We sent a large bundle with five copies of each Mandelstam book, plus some Nabokov. Our embassy acquaintance entered the spirit and gift-wrapped the large parcel, but then he made the mistake of entrusting it to his Soviet-provided Russian chauffeur to deliver it to her. Either the KGB or the black market or both had a bonanza. She never got the books, of course; and when Ellendea made her last visit in 1980, N. M. knew nothing of this present. The one copy of *Voronezh Notebooks* that Ellendea took was new to her, and made her very happy.

We had attempted to call her on that birthday, but without success, so we had sent this Western Union telegram: "Happy 80th birthday to Russia's greatest living writer. You have been an inspiration to us for 10 years now, you made Russian literature alive for us and all we have done since then has been an attempt to make it alive for others. We read and re-read your books and we urge others to read both Mandelstams. For your talent and courage we respect you. For your inspiration of us we thank you. We miss you very much. Love, C and E." Uncharacteristically sentimental and fulsome, but all true.

The most important present we ever gave to N. M. she gave back. Near the end of our 1969 visit Ellendea and I had acquired from a good Russian friend and great book collector ("Anything that depends on human beings I can get," he would say smugly) a copy of the first edition of Mandelstam's first book, *Stone (Kamen', AKME, 1913, 500 copies)*. Although he was used to handling rare books, our friend made a point of telling us that this *Stone* was really something special, incredibly rare; and it was one of only two times in our rare book conversations that he warned us: "You will not see this book again." We thought it was the appropriate going-away present for N. M. When we handed it to her in her kitchen, she smiled, said something about not having seen the actual book for some years, turned through the pages thoughtfully, recited a few lines, and then said, "You know— I know all these by heart. You take it back—you'll get more pleasure from it than I will."

None of us knew it then, but at that moment Ardis was founded. A year and a half later we decided to publish a new journal of Russian literature; then we decided to print some books too. *Stone* was the first book out under the Ardis imprint. We had reasoned that since she gave it to us, we could give it back to her in not one copy but in five hundred. So the thin but elegant facsimile brought Ardis into existence; it went through several printings and became a favorite of Russians everywhere.

Stone was the beginning, and since then almost a million books of and about Russian literature have been shipped from Ann Arbor to countries all over the world, but especially to the Soviet Union. All of the readers of Mandelstam, Akhmatova, Gumilev, Platonov, Erdman, Bulgakov, Nabokov, Brodsky, Sokolov, Bitov, Iskander, Aksyonov and dozens of others have that ostensibly powerless old lady on Cheryomushkinsky Street to thank for this: she was the catalyst for many things in our lives, her memory was the bridge between two eras, and she taught us some very special things about Russia.

We visited N. M. several times during the first Moscow Book Fair in September 1977. The Fair was unusually open, a result of detente. Even Voinovich and Kopelev, then both under fire, visited our stand. Only about 40 books were confiscated, even though all of the New York publishers had censored themselves in advance—this was a good sign. (That we were allowed to come surprised almost everyone.)

In connection with the Fair the American Embassy threw a party for the publishers and their guests at the house of Marilyn Johnson, a diplomat with a serious interest in culture. When asked to bring guests, we thought of asking N. M. just as a matter of principle. We did not think there was much chance that she would agree, because in all the years we had known her we had left her apartment with her only once. Nevertheless we asked her, explaining in detail what it was, and telling her that we thought it would be a good thing for her to make an appearance, not just for herself, but to be the representative of O. M. and the real Russian culture. Since she was in bed during this conversation, it was a surprise that she said she would go with pleasure.

Knowing the Kopelevs would also be at the party, we were somewhat apprehensive. Although we had met them at N. M.'s house, since the publication of *Hope Abandoned* they were among those who had not visited or spoken to her. (Lev had even wanted to have it out with me for my published "defense" of her, but Raya was more understanding of our feelings and she refused to let the subject come up.) We weren't sure which other writers might be present who had taken offense at N. M.'s books, or had been given offense in person.

Early on the day of the party we called to confirm that she still wanted to come and she did. We promised to pick her up. As it turned out, Vasily Aksyonov provided the car. He took us out to Cheryomushkinsky, and we drove over the tracks, around back of her apartment house and parked. He and I got out and walked straight in to get her. I rang the bell, but there was no response. I rang again a second and third time and still there was no answer. I was absolutely terrified, because considering her frailty and recent illness and the fact that we had agreed on the time just a few hours before, the first thing that occurred to me was that she had died. As I was frantically going over all the alternatives (wrong hour, she had been delayed somewhere, she was asleep, etc.), Ellendea came in and said that N. M. was waiting outside. It turned out that she had been waiting for us on the bench, just outside by the little car park. We simply didn't see her when we came in. Again the old lady was one step ahead of us.

Aksyonov drove us over to the isolated diplomatic buildings. When we arrived, the apartment was already crowded. N. M. took off her coat. Again we were surprised—she was quite fashionably dressed. She had on an elegant black sweater, a wool skirt, a nice scarf, and was all in formal black, with that same sense of style we had seen years before at the art exhibition.

As we circulated through the crowd, it became clear that virtually none of the publishers or embassy people had any idea who this old lady was, even after we introduced her. Besides the hostess the main exception was the then cultural attache, Jack Matlock. [He is now ambassador.] When we took her into a separate and quieter side room where she could sit peacefully, he talked to her at length.

Of course, the Russians who attended knew who she was and paid their respects. Besides Aksyonov, these included Vladimir and Ira Voinovich, the Kopelevs and many others. We were delighted that this went off without the trouble we had anticipated. And afterwards the Kopelevs both agreed that they had been wrong to have ended the friendship. Between 1972 and 1977 N. M. had changed drastically from a relatively robust and active person to a delicate wraith, weighing perhaps 90 pounds. When we met her, she was small, but still fairly solid, but as she got older and sicker she lost a great deal of weight. I was shocked to see how she looked in the fall of 1977, she was so frail; and when Ellendea saw her in 1980 she was even thinner. These years had not been good ones for her, and anyone who saw her in 1977 would naturally feel sympathetic. "People are more important than convictions," Raya Orlova Kopelev said. But it was not only sympathy that made these people respond to her that night. She was charming and, in a peculiar way, impressive simply as a presence.

N. M. tired easily but she stayed for more than an hour. Then, as agreed, I saw her back home again, using the official black car provided by the Soviets to the publishers. She would have been terrified if she had known, as I did, that I would have to sign the itinerary. In spite of the general ignorance on the American side, we thought it had been a good moment for her. If nothing else she had conquered her fear, and had enjoyed, I think, the sense of being someone in the world outside her apartment.

Besides our usual visits during the fair, I also took Winthrop Knowlton, then Harper & Row's president, out to meet her. We had decided to take someone from among the publishers, someone who had done a few Russian books and who seemed to have some real interest, and show him as much of cultural Moscow as we could. Win Knowlton had published Solzhenitsyn, and unlike most of our other colleagues, he was more interested in learning than in showing how much of an expert he was.

The sad thing that happened during his visit was that not long after we arrived (we had chatted with her for only a few moments) N. M. lapsed from lucidity into total confusion, of which she was unaware. I had no idea that she was intermittently senile, and I didn't know what to do. She confused Win and me and even asked him about my children. When I tried to explain who was who, she got further confused; and for much of the fifteen-minute visit she did not really understand things, even when she stayed on generally correct subjects. But then she shifted into normality and seemed very much the same old N. M. While I had seen the same phenomenon with a grandparent, I found it hard to recover from the shock. The thought of a mind like hers disintegrating was unbearable. I have no idea how often this kind of senility hampered her. I do know that in the contact we had subsequently nothing this serious was ever obvious. Thus, for example, when Ellendea visited her for the last time three years later, N. M. remembered the unusual name of our daughter (Arabella), whom she had seen only in pictures. In spite of further physical decline, she was also lucid about other topics.

I did not know it in 1977 but I was seeing N. M. for the last time— in 1979 because of the publication of the *Metropole* anthology, I would be declared *persona non grata* and never return to Russia.

We were depressed about almost everything connected to N. M. during the last few years we saw her. She had times of perfect lucidity, but gradually it became more difficult to talk seriously about anything. So our conversations became more predictable: we would bring her up to date on those in the emigration who interested her; she would comment on our news and perhaps tell a recent story or two. From her bed she would hoarsely lament the fate of the world, both the uncomprehending West and the cruel motherland. Her solace was in God and her Orthodoxy was more pronounced. Basically our regular visits served as affirmations of our affection for her. As her body withered away, her mind followed, even if at a distance. She could not have "conducted" the exciting salon of the past, even if she had wanted to. That she wrote her books when she did was a stroke of luck as well as genius. Occasionally there were wonderful flashes of the old

Nadezhda, but they grew rarer. We were just sad to see her sick. There were priests and a few old friends; and there were many old women who came in to help take care of her; but we saw mainly the grim signs of age. She would tell us we needed to believe in God too, that only He could save the world now. And she would mourn the murder of the Tsar. This was a shadow of Nadezhda Mandelstam. We thought of how terrible it would have been if she had emigrated. Most likely she would have ended up in England, and we could not imagine that there she would have had as many people as devoted to her as we saw here. She really had made the correct decision.

She had not been the "strong Russian woman," not the sacrificial Decembrist wife—indeed by psychology she was a girlfriend, not a wife. Elena Sergeevna Bulgakova could be the helper and manager for Bulgakov, she would always make sure the rent was paid on time; but Nadezhda did not have these resources. Yet she did everything she could for Mandelstam. She was little and did look Jewish—no help in Russian society. In her book she says she was weak and nobody believed it, but in many ways it was true. On the other hand, N. M. had been forced to do many things to hold together her everyday life with O. M., himself equally incapable of mundane tasks or heroes' feats. But intellectually she was repressed; she was supposed to keep quiet and hear what Akhmatova thought about sonnets. No doubt she made comments, but essentially she was containing things—including her anger and her pride. They burst loose only in her old age—and after she had to suffer much more deprivation and humiliation. Then, after O. M. died, came the years of begging (petitioning if you want to be polite). Begging to get this or that, begging to become an English teacher, begging to get a degree, begging to get a room, or begging to get into Moscow (and failing in 1958); and finally the begging worked and she got her dream—a two-room apartment in Moscow. And, it must be emphasized, this *was* a miracle—two rooms for *one* person, her own kitchen and bath. Westerners do not always recognize this for the achievement it is.

As she repeatedly said, she had hated teaching all the way from Chita to Pskov; for her, teaching meant attending meetings and abasing herself—as she had to do in other areas of her life, e.g., in getting her degree. Although she did all the work (very appropriately it was on the accusative case in early English), she was a suspicious character, the wife of that crazy O. M.; so the degree came only with a new kind of begging and abasement. As she said, a "gang" of them were against her, but "Zhirmunsky got his own gang" together and in the end she got the Candidate's Degree. Nothing was easy. She spent most of her life being underestimated, not having a place to call her own, forced into servility—and fear. Being forced to lie constantly made her bitter. During our very first meeting, she said: "We Russians are very great liars . . . I've been lying for years." And her friends were forced to lie about everything from their religion to the nature of art. I believe that her books were in some measure written to atone for all those years of lying. For the first time she could tell the truth as she saw it—and not the nice polite truth of other memoirists. It is that anger caused by years of lying, years of pent-up truth, that pours out of her books with such incredible power. And much of it is anger at herself, that she gave in.

We should all be grateful that the anger and the pride finally broke loose in her memoirs. It turned out that poor little "Nadya," witness to poetry, was also witness to what her era made of the intelligentsia: liars who lied even to themselves. She told much more of the truth about her life than Ehrenburg, Paustovsky, Kataev or anyone else could even dream of telling about theirs. She hadn't been in the camps, so she is no rival of Solzhenitsyn in describing them; but then neither was she warped and made narrow by the camps, so that her lessons for the world of writers and the intelligentsia in general are more valuable, it seems to me. And unlike Solzhenitsyn, when it came to what she put on paper, she never compromised. She never deleted a paragraph or changed a word in order to be published in the USSR. (Also unlike him, she never worried about being a member of the Union of Writers, and she never hoped to receive a Lenin Prize.)

While she sometimes described her memoirs to people as "just propaganda for Mandelstam," she knew quite well what they really were. She never said: look at me, see what I did; but she had a strong sense of her own worth. And once she had released her anger, she must have felt better. The world-wide acclaim, however muffled, and the stream of visitors were evidence of her external success; but we never heard her mention that. Nor did we ever hear her complain—after she was abandoned by so many for her *Hope Abandoned*—that she was unjustly treated. She liked flattery as much as anyone, but she never quite let herself believe it. Moreover, unlike many writers, she did not *require* it. While from style to specifics there was much to be praised in her books, we never felt that we had to keep telling her how great they were. Again, unlike many writers, she didn't ask whether her translators were as good as she was, how her book was doing in this or that translation, in this or that circle, what we thought of them, were they influential. She was much more interested in Mandelstam's success in the world, and her books were just part of that. When we published translations of his poetry, she was interested. When we published his *Complete Prose and Letters* and it won a National Book Award, she was incredibly pleased.

When Wayne Robart and Christine Rydel visited N. M. in 1976, she asked whether people in America really cared about O. M. After reassuring her of her husband's popularity, Christine told her a more personal anecdote. A student had come to ask Christine to direct an independent study of O. M.'s poetry, which, unfortunately, he could read only in translation. After a semester of study he enrolled in Russian language courses in order to read the poems in the original. Upon hearing this, N. M. began to weep; but smiling through the tears, she said, "Well, then, what I did was worth it."

1984

Elena Sergeevna Bulgakov

How does one measure power? Can one really believe that Nadezhda Mandelstam was a woman of great power? Is there any way in which she was typical? And finally, can one compare the power of Russian literary widows to the power of the official literary establishment—from the Central Committee through the Union of Writers down to the printing factories?

The first question is the hardest to answer, and since we need it to answer the last question, it is all the more crucial. One reasonable approach is to determine which writers are most read, which ones have the highest reputations, which are most published, or most translated. But again these are very different kinds of measure—there is no guarantee of correlation between numbers of books printed and a poet's reputation. Soon one has to start arguing whether all readers are equal, ask if reputation isn't formed by certain influential groups of readers (other writers, critics, scholars, teachers, dissertation writers), and of course the biggest question of all—where are the comparisons being made—in the Soviet Union, in the entire block of brotherly socialist countries, in the Third World, or in what we call the Free World of more or less advanced nations?

Bearing all this in mind, I would argue that Nadezhda Mandelstam was an extremely powerful woman, and that along with her the literary widows of Russia have had a strong and lasting effect on the history of Russian literature. Although in the short run the immense resources of the Soviet establishment enable it to set up and maintain its own territory, in the long run this huge puffball of pseudoliterature will disappear and the true literature will occupy its normal place.

Of course, it is ultimately the quality of the literature itself which makes this happen, but as I have had ample occasion to see even in my brief experience as a publisher and confidant of writers, great writers do not automatically occupy their rightful positions. They get there with time, because the right people (including everyone from already authoritative writers to publishers) talk and write about them, publicize them, propagandize them, insist on them, put them at the top in those lists which everyone professes to consider useless. The case of the "selling" of Joyce's *Ulysses* is instructive. In this complex sense, Nadezhda Mandelstam was a major force, and to varying extents the same can be said of other Russian widows. They do not work alone, of course, but they are primary sources which have great potential for power.

In spite of the vast government resources which are devoted to publicizing Soviet poets, I think it is reasonable to conclude that Mandelstam is far better known in most places of the world than such artificial classics as Tikhonov or Aseev. The role that Nadezhda Mandelstam played in the Mandelstam "boom" of the last fifteen years in America and Europe is easy to demonstrate. Soviets have desperately tried to make classics of Leonov and Fedin (so skillfully that E. J. Simmons followed their line precisely), two of their most ancient heroes (Leonov, still in Peredelkino, just celebrated his 85th anniversary; Fedin died in his eighties); but the great popularity and high reputation of, for example, Mikhail Bulgakov everywhere, including the USSR, shows how surely good literature drives out bad— and as I will demonstrate below, the roles played by Bulgakov's widows were by no means negligible in resurrecting him from near total oblivion at home and abroad.

If we close but do not lock the files containing Nabokov's convincing arguments about why all good biographies acquire an autobiographical character, and if we except such intentionally shadowy figures as B. Traven or Thomas Pynchon, we can assert that nothing is more perplexing than writing the biography of a Soviet writer. Where there is only one widow and she is as articulate as Nadezhda Mandelstam, at least the beginnings are simple. One starts there and does one's best to determine where the story is accurate and where it is inaccurate. But there are few interesting Soviet cases that give the scholar a reliable base to work from.

Much more common are the Soviet writers who had several wives. The wives were of varying temperaments, with memory tracks in various stages of disrepair. And quite a few of the writers themselves lied mercilessly about their past, to their wives as well as to interviewers from *Pravda, Red Virgin Soil* or *Red Pepper.* And in a nation of multiple revolutions, coups, and civil war, their mendacity was seldom literary mystification. A few writers played games, but most of them lied to save their skin—or increase its value. Parents of the wrong class, a period of service in the wrong army, or the ownership of too many horses were all grounds at one time or another for a bullet in the neck or confiscation of the family lands or apartment. So that one's birth certificate, academic history, party affiliations, etc. could keep one out of the "right-thinking" publications was no surprise. Trotsky's book *Literature and Revolution* helped popularize the term fellow traveller, and that is about as dirty a name as one wanted to be called.

Thus the ever-resourceful chameleon Babel censored from his personal history the whole first part of his writing career (1913-15), the especially dangerous second part (1917-19) when he published seventeen pieces in *The New Life* (a newspaper shut down by Lenin's order), and instead made it seem that good old safe Maxim Gorky had been his literary godfather, insisting that Gorky printed Babel's very first stories in *Chronicle* in November 1916, lying so successfully that his lies were repeated by every authority—Russian and English—until 1978! (I will deal with three of Babel's wives below, or at least with the three women by whom he begat children; he was successful in a way with them too.)

And in spite of his three wives (only one of whom is known to the general scholarly world), one of whom (Ludmila Nikolaevna) was repeatedly interviewed in free Paris, Evgeny Zamyatin remains an almost total mystery. He was born in 1884—and in this year when any other writer of his stature would be celebrating his centenary with the great acclaim, special collections, symposia, etc.—Zamyatin, so immensely successful with his secrecy, remains an enigma.

Pasternak's two wives and one mistress were bizarrely different in almost everything except their unreliability as witnesses. But at least in Pasternak's case, there was no secret—everybody in Moscow knew about all of the three, and the openly double life he led with his two final families was accepted by nearly everyone (indeed, it is a credit to his success as a Soviet writer that he was able to find housing for two different families). The last "wife" (mistress if you will) Ivinskaya has had her say at great and gushy length in *A Captive of Time,* but anyone who knows the Moscow scene realizes that her memoir has to be treated with extreme caution.

Bulgakov had three good wives. But in spite of no particular plot or attempt to keep this trilogy a secret, at the time of our research trip in 1969 it was the universal belief of the cognoscenti that Bulgakov had *one* wife, Elena Sergeevna Bulgakov, well known as the prototype for Margarita in his brilliant novel *The Master and Margarita* (written 1928-40, published 1966-73). Elena Sergeevna herself did not disabuse us innocent Americans of this monogamous notion. And why should she? Leading scholars accepted it honestly and unsceptically. It took us a few years and a few trips before the amazing news was liberated: Bulgakov had had a wife *before* Elena Sergeevna, a fact which emerged from a stage of embarrassment. A Bulgakov "evening" was held, a rare and exciting literary happening. The master-of-ceremonies waxed ecstatic over Bulgakov's soulmate, only wife, Elena Sergeevna, who had nurtured his imagination, served as his romantic prototype, and saved his archive. Moreover, she was present this very evening to receive his, and her, long overdue honor. However, Elena Sergeevna felt embarrassed by this one-sided view and commented that this was not the whole truth: in the audience sat Bulgakov's *previous* wife, Lyubov Evgenievna Belozerskaya, the very person to whom such works as the novel *White Guard* were clearly dedicated, in every edition. As if this were not enough, after another trip or two, it turned out that Bulgakov had a *still earlier* wife, from the Kiev days, Tatyana Lappa. Moreover, like Elena Sergeevna and Lyubov Evgenievna, she too was still alive.

Try to imagine the difficulties in establishing the chronology, details, and characters essential to a biography in a country where even such a basic and uncontroversial fact as this was "re-discovered" only thirty-five years after Bulgakov's death—even though all three widows had survived, two of them still in Moscow at the same addresses where he had lived with them! Imagine how difficult it was to get from such relatively uncontroversial material to such truly touchy matters as service in the White Army, attempts to emigrate, brief drug-addiction, and so on (all these true of Bulgakov). The whole story of how Ellendea's book *Bulgakov: Life and Work* was written is important because many of the obstacles Bulgakov's biographer had to overcome face every biographer of any Soviet writer of note, whether or not they have been officially accepted. In Bulgakov's case it was necessary to work in reverse chronological order, starting with Elena Sergeevna. This was the primary purpose of our first trip to Moscow in 1969. The rest of our meetings and our publications were serendipitous.

Again, for many topics, research done at the "official" level was far less important than that done unofficially. This was as true for

Bulgakov as it was for Osip Mandelstam. Of course, Bulgakov had not been "illegally repressed, posthumously rehabilitated" (the wonderful euphemism invented by the authoritative *Short Literary Encyclopedia*—in 9 volumes, 1962-78—for those who were arrested and killed). But Bulgakov was under suspicion all his life; he was subjected to secret police searches and interrogation, blacklisting, the banning of plays, and the confiscation of manuscripts. *None* of his major works was published in Russia after 1925. Not one of his plays was printed in his lifetime. For all practical purposes until the 1960s he was a nonperson. Therefore, any research on him was fraught with official and natural difficulties.

For example, since I was the official exchangee and had easiest access to the Lenin Library Manuscript Division, I could get Bulgakov books out—but there were virtually none to get out, and the journals containing his works had been censored—by tearing out his stories.

At the Manuscript Division (to which exchangees are admitted—if at all—only after long petitioning) I could submit all the requests for which I had energy, but like most foreigners I could get only a few items of interest. And, to give them some credit, they even photocopied a few items (access to copying machines is restricted). But most things were inaccessible, in part because of official policy on such a questionable writer, in part because one of the main powers in the Bulgakov section of the Manuscript Division at that time was Marietta Chudakova, and she wouldn't let *any* Bulgakov scholar—Russian or American—see documents of major significance, because she herself was preparing a book on Bulgakov. The official excuse was that the "archive is being put in order."

As in so many important cases, one had to work around the officially locked sources of information. It was the widows themselves who held the keys to so many mysteries. They had their own collections of papers; they had their own memories—and the specialists had to come to them. Finally, after the wives had waited for decades, the scholars did begin to come; and in the case of Bulgakov, we were among them. So we, like many others, have to express our gratitude for the incredible patience and faith of these women.

Nadezhda Mandelstam's phone call recommending us to Elena Sergeevna was very important; it is a good example of how the "widow network" worked. Nadezhda established our first level of worth and reliability. But we were unknown quantities, and we were Americans; perhaps these considerations made Elena Sergeevna decide to have us visit her with someone else first. Thus when we arrived for dinner, we were surprised to find that we were sharing the table with a rather well-known someone else—Vladimir Lakshin. Ellendea knew him mainly as a Bulgakov scholar, and together we knew him for the troubles then brewing around the editorial board of Tvardovsky's *Novy mir.* It was only a few years later that he was made famous, or rather, notorious, by Solzhenitsyn's hostile portrait in *The Oak and the Calf.* In the light of the conversation I had with him about Solzhenitsyn that evening, Solzhenitsyn's treatment of him is quite remarkable.

The main discussions he and I had were not about Bulgakov, but about Solzhenitsyn. I did not understand how close Lakshin was to the whole Solzhenitsyn matter (I didn't until Solzhenitsyn's book *The Oak and the Calf* came out), and I certainly had little idea of the huge battle that was then in progress over the very future of Solzhenitsyn in the USSR. But I had read Solzhenitsyn's early works, including *The First Circle.* (Indeed, I had written the Slavist Deming Brown, then in England, that I was going to try to get one of the two Russian copies of the novel which we had to Solzhenitsyn in Ryazan, though I don't remember how I expected to do that.) Anyway, I told Lakshin I thought *One Day in the Life of Ivan Denisovich* was good and original and "Matryona" good; but the miniature stories were hideous, and *The First Circle* was great for information, but that I couldn't imagine reading any of his novels more than once. Lakshin objected slowly but insistently: Solzhenitsyn was a great novelist, he was so great that none of us knew what we had working in our midst. "Another Dostoevsky?" I asked ironically. "Believe me, he is not worse than Dostoevsky," Lakshin answered, "or Tolstoi." He said all this in the tone of one who is utterly convinced and wants to convince you by his very calmness that he is correct. To the Solzhenitsyn argument, Elena Sergeevna added a story. Solzhenitsyn had been to visit her, she said, and the one thing she recalled Solzhenitsyn saying was that he was struck by Bulgakov's *imagination.* Solzhenitsyn remarked that he wrote almost exclusively about things that he had seen, that he *could not invent* things. But the *The Master and Margarita* showed so much imagination that he envied Bulgakov's ability to describe the fantastic. Elena Sergeevna was worldly and sophisticated. Even in her seventies she had a sexy quality. She was elegant, as was her apartment, although there was nothing stiff about it. She was a charming hostess.

Lakshin was also able to tell the middle part of a story which we had started in Moscow. Among the Bulgakov plays which Ellendea and I went to in our first months there was a production of *Flight* put on at the Ermolov theater. In it there is a famous speech by Korzukhin on the meaning of the all-powerful dollar. The speech is designed to show his crassness, and generally fits into the notion of Western capitalists as conscienceless money grubbers. As the actor performed this monologue he held up what was supposed to be a "dollar" to illustrate his speech. But the "dollar" was a large piece of wrong-colored cardboard. Ellendea and I thought this was very funny, especially when the Soviet theater brags so much about its realism. So I sat down and wrote a comically eloquent letter to the play's director about this matter, saying that in the cause of international friendship and artistic realism I was enclosing a brand new one-dollar bill which he could give to the prop department and use ever after during this monologue, arguing that this showed the dollar was not always used for evil ends. We didn't really expect an answer, but a week later a message was delivered to us in room 310 of the Hotel Armenia, where we lived, by a messenger who had arrived on a motorcycle. We were already celebrities at this ancient hotel (which generally had no foreigners of any kind, let alone Americans), but this proved our importance beyond question to the staff. On an official blank of the theater, dated March 7, 1969, came the reply:

Most respected Mr. Professor!

I am happy that as an expert on and translator of Bulgakov you like our production.

We are touched by your friendly desire to strengthen the veracity of the details of Korzukhin's monologue on the dollar and have passed your gift on to the prop department. If he were alive, perhaps Bulgakov would write a new monologue on the dollar, which in the hands of honest artists, in certain circumstances, can be transformed from a means of hostility into a sign of friendship.

Best wishes and greetings to your wife.
With respect,
V. Komissarzhevsky

All of this seemed in the same comic vein I had started, but Lakshin told us it had not all been that funny. According to him, when they opened the envelope the dollar fell out first. Immediately Komissarzhevsky called for witnesses to gather around—perhaps this was some sort of provocation prepared by the Americans (it is against the law for Soviets to possess hard currency). They were genuinely upset at first, and only after reading the letter did they decide that it wasn't a trick, but just what it appeared to be. In any case, it was remarkable enough an event to spread quickly through the Bulgakov circles. Lakshin was now amazed to discover the perpetrator: "so it's *you* who did that."

After dinner Elena Sergeevna showed us around the apartment featuring the Bulgakov iconography: the death mask in a cabinet, photographs everywhere, the bed where he had slept and died. We were extremely touched, and hardly knew how to react. After all, it was in order to see this kind of inner sanctum that we had come to the Soviet Union in the first place, and our only regret was that it was already June 10 and we would not get to do much more. And while we realized Elena Sergeevna was not telling us everything she might, we withheld things from her as well—such as the fact that we already had the 1935 Russian text of *Zoya's Apartment,* and had lines on a variety of other rare or unknown Bulgakov materials. I suspect that if she had lived another five years, things might have been different; once we had established a relationship, and Ardis developed as rapidly as it did, she might have been more willing to go beyond the careful limits she adhered to until 1969.

Although she was easily the most glamorous and charming of them, her role was like that of many of the widows. In 1969 she was the first source: she had collected the papers and saved the books, she had the archive. The student who wanted to know something would have to come to her if things were to be easy—otherwise the amount of work to be repeated was huge. She had devoted much of her life after 1940 to the preservation of Bulgakov's name, in a way he himself had predicted. She had been very careful about keeping the important manuscripts locked up. Not very many people knew about them. Bulgakov's manuscripts did not generally circulate in samizdat, and that was obviously Elena Sergeevna's doing. On the whole she—rather like Tamara Ivanova—had held back, waiting for the "real day" to come. As we have seen, to an extent her tactics were good, and that real day did come. *The Master and Margarita* was an instant classic in Russia. It was soon translated into nearly every major language and the availability of the uncut version may well have been her doing.

Spousal censorship in Russia is at least as old as Dostoevsky's second wife; she not only used a rare and fiendish kind of shorthand for her diary, she also made a couple of passes through it to blot out details she considered too compromising or intimate. Elena Sergeevna did not (as far as we know) destroy things that were headed for the archives, but she spilled ink strategically over some sections she thought not even posterity should be permitted to read.

In any event, Elena Sergeevna was one of the important literary widows of Russia. Whether or not we agree with her tactics (which sometimes included donating other relatives' letters from Bulgakov to the archives *without* their permission), it is clear that she played a very important role in Bulgakov's posthumous career. If it had been left completely to others, to friends, many of whom were very cowardly, or others like Ermolinsky and Mindlin, who were capable of remembering all kinds of non-existent events and purposely lying about many things, the Bulgakov heritage would be far poorer. One clear example of the complexity of the "politics of knowledge" about Bulgakov is his late play about the young Stalin. Certainly Elena Sergeevna, who had a copy of *Batum* (1938), would never have authorized its release because (aside from her possible role in its creation) it does tend to make Bulgakov look bad. It puts him in the company of so many other great writers who stooped to praise Stalin. Thus one hagiographic memoirist would never release his copy, and even the person who did eventually procure a copy of the play for Ellendea suggested it would be best not to publish it—people would misunderstand Bulgakov. And while that view is understandable, it is still fortunate that in the end the truth (i.e., the text) was made known.

Elena Sergeevna had not reached this stage of freedom, but it is very hard for anyone—especially one who has survived the Soviet experience—to reach it. That is why Nadezhda Mandelstam was so remarkable. However, no one worked harder to keep the Bulgakov flame alive and the image attractive than Elena Sergeevna did. And when the day came that the ban on Bulgakov was finally lifted, however carefully, selectively, and mendaciously, the work she had done represented the first stage of knowledge, the first source.

1984

Lyubov Belozerskaya. Photo: Wayne Robart.

Lyubov Evgenievna Belozerskaya

Once we learned that Bulgakov had not one but three living widows, we made more than the usual haste to try to make contact with the others. We never managed to meet the first wife, although a trusted friend did manage to send us a copy of a short and revealing interview with her. (It may be a rule that candor and chronological position are in inverse relationship.) And eventually this widow's testimony will come out. Even as I write this, Lappa's recollections, preserved on dozens of cassettes, are being considered for publication in the West. A copy of her memoirs is certainly resting in a Soviet archive, other copies are also in other places. Since at least one is outside the USSR, we do not have to worry about important information being totally destroyed by or proscribed for a long period by the cautious Soviet officials in charge of literary history.

In between the first and last wives we have the mixed case of Lyubov Evgenievna Belozerskaya, to whom several works by Bulgakov were dedicated: *White Guard, Molière, Heart of a Dog.* In spite of her name in the dedication to *White Guard,* Lyubov's existence was almost totally unknown until that evening which I have described above. This is typical of the Russian sense of propriety—which often means a belief in hagiographic cover-up. Fortunately, once this particular cat was out of the bag, the amount of information about one of the basic periods (Moscow 1924-32) of Bulgakov's life increased exponentially. This was due to Lyubov Evgenievna's willingness to share parts of what she knew with the world. One suspects that the fact that Soviet scholars and Soviet officials had ignored her existence for years played a role in her decision to help not only Russian Bulgakov scholars, but foreigners such as ourselves. By the time we knew of her existence, found a mutual friend, and arranged to meet, our efforts to build

Bulgakov's English reputation were substantial: we had translated and published two volumes (early plays and stories) and Ellendea's dissertation (finished in 1970) was easily the most detailed study of Bulgakov's life and works in any language; so it was obvious from the moment we met that we had a considerable community of interests. And Ellendea knew exactly what to ask, although she did not always get candid answers.

Again, to our surprise, it turned out that Lyubov Evgenievna was still living in the same building (though not in the same apartment) in which she had lived with Bulgakov before he left her for her friend Elena Sergeevna, under very difficult circumstances. In terms of wealth, she was somewhere between Elena Sergeevna and Nadezhda Mandelstam, but closer to Elena Sergeevna—and we assumed the rooms reflected Bulgakov's relative wealth at the time he lived there almost fifty years before. (The extent to which Russia is a non-mobile society never ceased to amaze us.) Thus, the building, and the apartment, were older and not in good shape, but still quite respectable. Lyubov Evgenievna had one main room where we did nearly all of our talking and reminiscing. A large table was in the center, bookcases were along one wall, and a worn couch along another. The most noticeable feature of all this, for the first-timer especially, was the presence of a multitude of cats. Lyubov Evgenievna really likes cats, and we never counted; but there were enough so that some were always under foot, and the smell never went away. We weren't sure we liked so many cats together, but we managed to get used to them, their odor, and the flies which filled the place in warmer weather.

Lyubov Evgenievna had lost little of her sharpness with age; we never had the feeling we had to talk down to her or work hard to get anything straight. She was intelligent, a warm hostess (even though she had not the financial means of Elena Sergeevna or Lily Brik), and another widow who really understood how things work in the Soviet Union. One who not only knew, but had figured it out a long time ago. Even though the resurrection of Bulgakov had begun, it was a partial resurrection, and in many ways a false one. Moreover, it was one which had totally omitted her; and she was not about to be passed over again. It was one thing to lose Bulgakov to Elena Sergeevna, but quite another to sit in silence, while the official establishment made pilgrimages to the charming Margarita-prototype and totally ignored the clever young woman who had gotten Bulgakov through one of the hardest periods of his life. At least on the period from *The Days of the Turbins* to *Molière,* she was going to have her say.

For example, Elena Sergeevna did not feel the need to write memoirs. She could easily have written them—as Tamara Ivanova and many others did. She had years to do so. But on the one hand, that was not her interest—Bulgakov and his texts were her interest; and on the other hand, once the door opened, Elena Sergeevna was the one standing there. She had an irreproachable Soviet background, and she could easily serve as the official representative of Bulgakov and his works. She had the wit, intelligence, and knowledge to deal with the conservatively formed literary commission on the preservation of the heritage of the works of M. A. Bulgakov. Besides, her diaries were there in the archives, and one day would provide her words for the story. Elena Sergeevna was firmly in the picture.

But Lyubov had been left out. First her existence had been denied. Then when it was discovered, it was something of an embarrassment. So while a few true scholars made their way to Bolshaya Pirogovskaya to see what the "other" woman had to say, her role was definitely secondary. Not many of the few scholarly articles written at this time made reference to her. It would be another decade before there was much official acknowledgment that she existed, so it was no wonder she was willing to talk to experts from abroad.

The main result of our friendship was her memoirs. We published the Russian and the (slightly edited) English version of these; and we believe (though we have never seen the book) that they were printed in Yugoslavia from our text. This book is one of the basic books of early Bulgakoviana, not just for Bulgakov's biography, but for his works. And while like most other books in this genre it contains some information of little interest and glaring lacunae, it fills in a great deal of important information about one vital period. And, for the whole world, it is information which is available *now*, not 30, 50 or 200 years from now. Lyubov Evgenievna took one of the other routes, used one of the other strategies—not waiting for official policy to come around, but making the truth about the past known in her own lifetime—and doing so in spite of possible risk to herself, although her memoirs did not contain anything about the political world, as Nadezhda Mandelstam's did.

Unlike Nadezhda Mandelstam, Lyubov Evgenievna did not talk about fear; she had some fear of retaliation (perhaps with her pension, or apartment) but she didn't talk about it much. And we suggested from the start that we doubted a woman of her age was likely to get in trouble with officials because of this book—which, after all, has extremely minimal political content. Still, it is interesting that Lyubov

Evgenievna's temperament was such that she was willing to forge ahead. This sort of daring went along with surface gentility. For example, she was disinclined to say anything about her rivals, such as Elena Sergeevna; but in time, when asked the right kind of provocative question, her sharpness would come out. This was the only way one could get her to say truly personal things, or get into the whole area of her personal relations with Bulgakov or "her friend." As she put it, Elena Sergeevna "came into this house as my friend." When A. C. Wright's book came out, she was horrified by the "gossip" in it. In March 1980 she wrote us urging that Ellendea's book not be like this, "including everything," she heard.

Thus, on the whole Belozerskaya's *My Life with Bulgakov* is rather soft in tone; and she is innocent of structure like many first-book authors. But while some of the details she gives are uninteresting, read carefully by one who knows Bulgakov's life and work, her memoirs are a valuable source.

Lyubov Evgenievna had also built a collection of Bulgakov materials. Bulgakov's reputation outside the Soviet Union was a continuing interest, and she kept close track of Soviet publications. She had a number of family photographs and various other items of iconography (some used in her book) which she gathered, along with manuscripts or bits of manuscripts from her years with Bulgakov. For example, we assume she had a number of letters, although she never allowed us to see anything substantial. (She was the one who told us that after Lappa's remarriage, Lappa destroyed all vestiges of her relation with Bulgakov, including all of his photographs and letters—a truly devastating loss for scholars.) In the case of works dedicated to her, she had texts. She showed us some very important variants of one play, for example, and the real ending of another.

We discussed with her truly sensitive matters such as Bulgakov's intentions about emigration. Here she was not altogether forth-coming, since other evidence showed that Bulgakov tried quite hard to leave. However, in her memoirs Lyubov Evgenievna insists that Bulgakov did not ask to emigrate. In the narrowest sense, this may be true: possibly he did not use the dangerous word "emigrate," but it is difficult to believe that he did not at least use the general line he had taken in previous letters to the "Government of the USSR": since I am banned and useless here, either send me out for as long as you wish or give me some literary work. Lyubov Evgenievna does not explain what the "March" letter to Stalin asked, and she says nothing about the published September 3 and 29, 1929 letters to Gorky in which Bulgakov clearly asks to be sent abroad.

In her memoirs Lyubov Evgenievna intentionally avoids the whole dangerous truth about this issue (as she "smooths over" other sensitive issues—not just those involving divorce). Thus on the one hand she was bold enough to take the "foreign" route, but on the other, she followed most Russian memoirists' practice of avoiding the hard questions.

Lyubov Evgenievna's attempt to whitewash Bulgakov is not too different from efforts by other widows to make their husbands seem acceptable to Soviet power—including Elena Sergeevna's. Currently Lyubov Evgenievna is supposedly preparing to publish a second volume of memoirs with a Soviet publishing house, and they said no words of reproach to her for the first book. If by some miracle her second volume does appear in the USSR, it will certainly be censored and follow the same general line of optimism and loyalty that is true of all printings of Soviet classics.

Again this is very typical of the Soviet process. After Elena Sergeevna's death, when she could no longer "reproach" one (although she would never have done so) for going to Lyubov Evgenievna, the latter became the official widow. She wrote Ellendea a letter in January 1979 which clearly shows the changing situation. Lyubov Evgenievna describes how on December 18, 1978, *she* was invited to the premiere of *Days of the Turbins* in Orel at the Turgenev Theater. She says the actors were all "in love with" Bulgakov. "The theater invited me to the premiere. I was met with extraordinary *warmth* [her emphasis], with ecstasy even. The warmth of the troupe was in sharp contrast to the temperature outside—over 30 degrees of frost." What is important here is that now *she* is the respected guest, she is the widow in her rightful place, surrounded by love for Bulgakov. Obviously, this has to change one's notion of one's self and one's role in the resurrection of a dead writer—including whether it should be done abroad for a few thousand libraries or at *home,* where the Turgenev Theater and others like it will play out their respects.

Lyubov Evgenievna felt free to criticize Bulgakov's works while she was with him, but Elena Sergeevna literally worshipped Bulgakov's talent. Naturally, this attitude pleased the writer. Elena Sergeevna, who had very high-level contacts, was more of a realist in her attitude toward Soviet literary power; thus she played the game, a waiting game, and had many successes. Lyubov Evgenievna found this less congenial a role; in writing her memoirs she did not cover up the

1926 search by the secret police and the confiscation of Bulgakov's manuscripts and diaries. She could make fun of it in a way, but she knew the meaning of all this for Bulgakov's career. And she freely mentions the unmentionable work—*Heart of a Dog*—which Soviet critics cannot *name* now. While Elena Sergeevna did not talk about it to us, she took the brave step of carrying the manuscript of *Heart of a Dog* to France for publication. Like Elena Sergeevna, Lyubov Evgenievna had been abroad; and she learned permanently the difference between the world "outside" and the new one inside. But each widow chose her own course to follow; both of them fell far short of the candor (not to mention talent) of someone as strong as Nadezhda Mandelstam, but in her own way each played an important role in the resurrection of the life and works of Bulgakov.

1984

Lily Brik

Of course, the accepted classics have widows too, and they have sometimes been strong forces. One of the most striking cases is that of Lily Brik, unofficial wife of Mayakovsky. It was her letter to Stalin in 1935 that worked the magic of changing Mayakovsky from a dubious individualist suicide into *the* Soviet classic poet. In the margin of Lily's letter Stalin wrote the magic words: "Comrade Brik is right: Mayakovsky is and remains the most talented poet of our Soviet epoch. Indifference to his memory and works is a crime."

This was clearly one of the great flukes in literary history. It is inconceivable that if Stalin had leisure time his reading pleasure included the one-time Futurist's ambiguous lyrics. Stalin *had* been struck by Mayakovsky's suicide in 1930, but it is doubtful that he had given Mayakovsky a lot of serious thought since 1930. But Lily's letter in which she expressed fear that Mayakovsky's memory was in danger prompted Stalin's unexpected certification of Mayakovsky's greatness—following which monuments rose all over Russia, and everything from farms to forges was named after Mayakovsky. A whole Mayakovsky industry tooled up, complete with scholarly editions, specialist critics, obligatory school readings, college reading lists, dissertations, museums, and so on. While Stalin was alive no one risked the crime of ignoring Mayakovsky.

But after Stalin died, the Mayakovsky industry did start to slow down, and it grew more complicated. For years Lily Brik had been the semi-official, primary source of information; and many of the Mayakovsky stories and lines originated with her, both at home and abroad. By no means did this end with Stalin's death, but gradually challenges were issued.

When Ellendea and I began our regular visits to Moscow it was

Lily Brik. Photo by Wayne Robart.

not long before we were brought to the apartment of Lily Brik and her last husband (and Mayakovsky expert), Vasily Katanyan. As was so often the case, Lev Kopelev and Raisa Orlova were the ones who arranged the meeting, and they accompanied us on our "maiden" voyage to the Brik (never the "Katanyan") apartment off Kutuzovsky Prospect.

Because we were accustomed to the matter-of-fact poverty of Nadezhda Mandelstam and to the relative lack of prosperity of our friends, this initial visit to Lily's apartment struck us in many ways. It was many times more luxurious than Elena Sergeevna's as well. Spacious by Soviet standards, it had a large formal library (full of Mayakovsky necessities, old and new), an entranceway, hall, and living room richly decorated with original Futurist and Constructivist paintings and posters, including works by Malevich, Burlyuk, and Mayakovsky himself, notably his self-portrait in oils, hung opposite the table in the living room. The Tyshler painting of Lily was in the bedroom. Good, but not sumptuous furniture, real carpets, a wealth of objects everywhere—every place seemingly covered, not all with original art, but nevertheless a plethora of *things* of the sort that Nadezhda Mandelstam had never had in her life, despite the fact that she had started out as an art student. Even the bathroom was decorated—quite unusual in our experience of anything less than the party elite. Lily had a huge collection of kitschy trays from all over Russia. An awful rug featuring a raised duck was hung on the wall—a gift from Mayakovsky, who, like Lily, enjoyed humorously bad art.

The heavy table, covered with a nice starched tablecloth, was overflowing with potables and eatables. Just when we were full and assumed that the eating was over, Lily gave a sign and a parade of formal courses began, all borne in sequence from an invisible kitchen by an efficient woman servant. And it was lucky that we had come dressed formally, because Lily obviously appreciated such things; and she herself was always elegantly dressed and made up. She took pains—one could not have dyed the long braid she had without a lot of trouble. We remembered how Mayakovsky dressed and posed for every photograph.

Ellendea and I were humorous about all this in our moments alone together. Lily was near ninety, and her red hair and penciled eyebrows had their grotesque side and reminded one of Pushkin's Countess in "The Queen of Spades." Her spirit and sharpness were enviable, however.

Our visits to Lily and Vasily were always conducted along the same pattern, with a major meal a necessary prelude to most business matters. Lev and Raya were a wonderful help in breaking the ice the first time, and later on one or the other often accompanied us. At the time of our first visit in 1972, when we were planning the two-volume *Russian Literature Triquarterly* on contemporary writing, we intended to open it with a tribute to four or five poetic classics of the past—one of whom would be Mayakovsky. We tended to talk mainly about Mayakovsky: his poetry, his life, her life with him as well as what *we* could do by way of translations or Russian publications to publicize him in the U.S. and England.

It was quite important to her, I think, that when we came to her we were already publishers, that we had Russian interests and could do literally anything that it occurred to us to do. It was important that we had reprinted Mayakovsky's *Tragediia (Tragedy)* and brought her copies. Ellendea thinks Lily also liked me because I was tall, but I discount the importance of that in the repetition of the invitations. In any case we never had the kind of close personal relationship with Lily that we did with Nadezhda Mandelstam and a few others. But oddly enough, there was *something* between us, despite her narcissistic inability to truly connect with people. She spoke very openly with each of us—especially when Katanyan left the room. It would have been impossible for us to be real friends, probably because we knew too much about Lily's past from many sources, who considered her a symbol of the worst aspects of truly "Soviet" literature. While our curiosity, scholarly instincts, and the sheer wonder of talking to this figure of the past kept us fascinated, we found it hard to forget the Muscovite stories of the Briks' salon and its many Cheka regulars in the 1920s. All of this was a long time ago, and certainly, Lily had merely been true to her own belief in the Revolution. Ellendea even asked her directly how she and Mayakovsky and Brik could have closed their eyes to what was happening: "It was freedom, it was the Revolution, we saw it only as good; we knew of the murders and so on, but we thought it inevitable—excesses would occur, but they were part of the great liberation. It was exciting, and we were young." This was said with full acknowledgment of the fact that they had been wrong to have been so blind.

It was hard not to notice the obvious differences between someone like Nadezhda Mandelstam and Lily. Partly because of her sister Elsa Triolet and the powerful French Communist writer Louis Aragon, Lily had even been allowed to travel abroad. She kept up on the avant-garde even then—in Italy (Pasolini) and at home

(Paradzhanov). Lily's life had certainly had its bad times, but compared to Nadezhda Mandelstam's, it had been wonderful. She had been on the right side in 1917, she had picked the right poet to hitch her star to, she had had powerful secret policemen as friends. Compared to the average Russian, she—because of Mayakovsky—had been rich and favored most of her life, and Nadezhda Mandelstam—because of Mandelstam—had been the opposite. Or at least that was how it looked to us.

This was also reflected in a comparison of the resources. Nadezhda Mandelstam had few books or manuscripts; her mind and memory were her main resources. On the other hand, Lily—and Katanyan—had a very large library and a substantial cache of unpublished materials. So far as we know there was nothing as potentially exciting as a trove of unpublished Mayakovsky, poems or original works by other Futurists or LEF supporters. But there were many letters, original manuscripts which had not been reproduced, photographs, albums and so on, as well as the research library itself. Lily had many stories to tell, and Katanyan was finishing his own extensive study of Mayakovsky. In many ways Lily was stronger and braver than Katanyan, and kept him going, despite the fact that she was older.

Lily and Katanyan provided some interesting materials which we published in *Russian Literature Triquarterly,* notably photographic items (photos of a Khlebnikov letter and a Mayakovsky letter to her, and a poem, a photo of Mayakovsky's ring for her with the infinitely repeating *Lyublyu*), mostly used in the Futurist-Contructivist issues (nos. 12 and 14). She also gave us photographs of two unknown Rodchenko montages; they had been planned for the initial edition of Mayakovsky's *Pro eto (About That),* but were omitted—so they appeared for the first time in our reprint of the book. Other foreign scholars, all with far more knowledge and interest in Futurism than we, also visited her regularly; and the results of their efforts have also been published, mainly in Scandinavia. The most interesting of these was undoubtedly the fairly extensive Brik-Mayakovsky correspondence, which was published in 1983, after her death. But the sad fact is that even their correspondence is on the whole pretty boring. Indeed, it's mainly interesting for showing how passionless and businesslike relations between them had grown—a far cry from the heated metaphor of "The Backbone Flute." But I suspect that from Lily's point of view the main thing was to keep a steady stream of materials about Mayakovsky coming—abroad if not at home—and especially materials that showed Lily as a major figure, which she certainly was. Curiously, she repeatedly told Ellendea: "He really loved me, you know," but never put it the other way around. She had been a great beauty, was quite bright, but Ellendea had the sense that this woman had never loved anyone. In Nadezhda Mandelstam one could still see passion; in Elena Sergeevna even sexiness—but not in Lily. A good Muse, but not a good lover. She did love the memories of herself, however. There were many pictures of herself in the apartment, one of which she gave to me, nicely inscribed.

An especially virulent attack on her role as the font of Mayakovsky information was the subject of several meetings. We found Lily and Katanyan extremely upset and anxious for advice. The sycophant poet Smelyakov had written a long diatribe proving that Lily and "the Jews" had been keeping "the real Mayakovsky" from the people all these many decades. Some of it was too vile even for Soviet publication, but part of it was printed in a well-known journal. She gave us a copy of the whole essay, hoping we would find a place to publish it and stop the attacks. We sent it to various Western Mayakovsky scholars, who thought it best unanswered.

From our point of view, the most interesting thing Lily had was a complete fair copy in Pasternak's hand of his great book *My Sister—Life*. When she first mentioned it, and we expressed great excitement, Lily took us into her bedroom, where she kept special treasures in a small chest. Pasternak's handwriting was always beautiful and large, but this manuscript was a particularly fine example; and more important, the copy he had made and given to Lily differed from the published version in many details, including epigraphs and text. They immediately agreed to let us photograph her manuscript and publish it. They were surprised we thought it should be made available to a larger audience; but photography was not my strong suit, especially when it meant getting every page lit evenly. It turned out to be rather difficult for an amateur, and I never managed to get it all. (The final version, not quite complete, will be published, however.)

Lily tried to get us to publish various other things. The most revealing project was Chernyshevsky's *What is to Be Done?* She described it with great enthusiasm (and as if we wouldn't have heard about it), and said she was sure if we published it in English, it would be a great commercial success. The sexual mores preached by Chernyshevsky, the potential three-way affairs (supposedly practiced by Mayakovsky and the Briks) had made a great impression on her—she told Ellendea that it had been an important book for her life.

In purely human terms, the most interesting thing which came from Lily was the remarkable story of Mayakovsky's unknown daughter—born to an American Communist sympathizer, conceived during an affair they had during Mayakovsky's visit to the United States and Mexico in 1925. This sensitive subject came up during our conversations about Mayakovsky's loves. Tatyana Yakovleva was the starting point, and it was an interesting coincidence, we said, that she was married to Alexander Liberman of *Vogue*, and lived right across the street from our good friends in New York, Arthur and Elaine Cohen. Along the same line, we said, but more mysterious, was an incident in California, where we had been with Joseph Brodsky. An old friend of ours walked up to us after a reception and said with a conspiratorial smile: "Do you know you were just in the same room with one of Mayakovsky's lovers?" We didn't, and he wouldn't explain further. Lily got quite excited about this, and asked us if we knew that Mayakovsky had a daughter who was conceived while he was in America, and about whom very little was known, indeed. She herself had no information except that which was very old. Katanyan was clearly unhappy that she had mentioned this, and he kept trying, ineffectively, to keep her from giving any more details. But we kept asking questions, and Lev and Raya did as well, and Lily got more and more intrigued by the old secret and thought that we might just be able to solve the riddle and find out the present name and location of this illegitimate daughter, if she had survived beyond the twenties. Her deep feeling for Mayakovsky and her sense of responsibility to his heirs was striking in all this. She had no jealousy about any of the women discussed, and seemed, rather, to have a sense of community with them.

While Vasily Abgarych sputtered, Lily went and got a packet of cards and letters from the 1920s, written by the mother to Mayakovsky, in each case signing the name "Elly Jones." Lily started reading them to us; then I started to copy down crucial addresses and dates, and even a few parts of the text—before Vasily Abgarych finally persuaded her to be more cautious and put them away. (I had managed to get a few in my hands, and copy things into a little notebook as she went on talking.) We assumed that the daughter might have been lied to all her life, and should be as proud as she would be shocked to discover who her real father was. Lily decided to help further by providing a drawing of "Elly Jones" done by David Burlyuk in 1925, and we have this drawing in the Ardis archives.

It depicts a so-called "Elizaveta Alekseevna," under which is written "Mrs. Jones." It was drawn in the fall, "at camp Nitgedaget with Mayakovsky." A little research when we returned revealed that this was in fact a well-known Jewish leftist camp, and Mayakovsky had been there at this time.

According to Lily, the illegitimate daughter of Mayakovsky was born to this "Elizaveta Aleksevna" or "Mrs. Jones," if we go by the drawing. In the cards and letters from Elly to Mayakovsky, written between the summer of 1926 and the end of 1929, the presumed mother signs herself variously, and it is clear that the "Jones" is a code name or pseudonym. The crucial communication came on May 6, 1926; she wrote Mayakovsky asking that $600 be sent "for the hospital" within three weeks. If Lily is correct about the pregnancy, presumably this means the baby was due in late May or early June 1926. Therefore the conception was precisely during Mayakovsky's visit in 1925. The return address on this letter is "195 27th St. Apt. F32, Jackson Heights, NY." Another letter was sent shortly thereafter. The return address on this one, perhaps one of the most important, is precisely as follows: "Mrs. Elly Jones / c/o Col. Walton H. [or N?—CRP] Bell / 25 W. 45th St. /New York City." On July 20, 1926, "Elly" sent another letter, this one also with the Jackson Heights return address. The only phrases I was able to copy were these: "Bert will get free in August . . . I am sure that we will all get visas." She also says, "Pat is with me—she's been with me all this time." If she did have a baby around June 1, it sounds like "Pat" was helping to care for mother and child. It also sounds like Bert, she, and possibly others have applied for visas to visit Russia.

The only other specific information I could copy was from cards or letters dating from November 1928 and April 1929. There is one written November 8, 1928 and postmarked Nov. 9, 1928 with the return address "Elly Jones / 16 Ave Shakespeare / apt 25 / Nice, France." In this Elly notes that Tina Zhdanova and Susanna Marr are her friends. Another letter dating from this same time, according to Lily, contained photographs, which Lily showed us, including a photo of a little girl—Mayakovsky's child.

The next missive in this major mystery (that I have an actual hard quotation from) is dated April 12, 1929. It is a letter to Mayakovsky signed "Elizaveta Petrovna" [not Alekseevna as in the Burlyuk drawing], and it says, among other things: "And you know, write this address in your address book under the heading: In the event of my death among others I request that among those informed be—us." This is followed by the Elizavetna Petrovna signature *and* the same address of Colonel Walton Bell in New York City (25 W. 4th St) that had been used earlier. This ominous letter comes a year before Mayakovsky's suicide, but since Mayakovsky was still young and in fine health, one must conclude that Elly either had a remarkable presentiment—or had been told by Mayakovsky what his mood was and how he might end.

The last item I was able to make a note on was dated April 19, 1929 and this communication had the return address "Mme Elly Jones/Covingham Rd/Golders Green/London NW 11" on it. If my notebook entries are in correct order, this one includes the statement that "someone (Bert) had been proposed by Longacre Construction Co. to go to Russia."

I presume that all of these documents disappeared into the deepest holds of the manuscript division of either the Lenin Library or TSGALI in Moscow after Lily's death. Whether anyone else was given further information about "Elly Jones" I doubt, given Katanyan's strenuous objections; but we cannot possibly expect Soviet scholars to deal with this for many decades.

Ellendea and I made some efforts to pursue this matter, and ran into a good deal of hostility, partly because anything coming from Lily was deemed suspect, partly because the possible women included very well-known persons. The daughter exists, or existed, we are fairly certain of that. She may or may not have been raised by the mother. She is probably unaware of who her father was.

As it happens I have a pretty good idea of the identity of Elly Jones; but I have not followed up all of the details which should be checked and I do not know what happened to the daughter herself. If I am right, the mother is still alive.

And a final note: in Russia it is more or less taken for granted that poets are sexually active more than the average person. Thus, one could argue, perhaps Elly Jones was not the only one who bore a little Mayakovsky, and that it is of no more importance than Chekhov's boast about leaving little Chekhovs on Ceylon. Nevertheless, in an era when important poets did not leave many descendants, intentionally in some cases, since the post-revolutionary period did not impress them as an era in which to raise a normal family, the discovery of a true descendant of Mayakovsky would not be without interest.

It is also of some interest that Lily Brik herself should tell this story—strongly against the wishes of Vasily Abgarych, and only in our case probably because we mentioned some possible knowledge of a woman in America who had been with Mayakovsky. Lily herself never bore a child, and we never heard of any Mayakovsky children. But it is typical that she was the open one, the one less afraid of scandal—or some kind of competition. Lily was a very sharp-witted old woman. She didn't have it in her to write the kind of books Nadezhda Mandelstam did, but she still had all of her faculties functioning well, and I don't think she made mistakes in such matters. There was something very novelistic, however, about sitting with an old woman in Moscow and imagining what Mayakovsky's daughter would look like, and wondering where—and if—she lived.

What can be said by way of summary of Lily Brik? We were impressed by her strength. In spite of her age, like many of the other widows we knew, she still had a good mind. No doubt one reason for this was the need to keep the memory of her poet alive (and of course along with it her own). She still had a sense of humor, an enjoyment of kitsch. She still kept up on art, was an active defender of the director Paradzhanov (then jailed for homosexuality), an admirer of contemporary poets such as Sosnora. We saw numerous examples of her generosity, to others and to us. Not the least was once when she was showing us a kind of scrapbook, which was filled with primitive drawings by Kamensky (an early Russian pilot and futurist poet), who had damaged his right arm in a plane crash, but did a whole album of crayon drawings with his left hand and gave it to her. I was especially touched by this, and by the motif of the airplane which occurred in several, and she just tore out a couple, including one of the plane, and gave it to me. The museum which she had made of her apartment was really quite well done, a good mixture of things which were important and things which had significance for her, or her and Mayakovsky together; and her artistic sense could be seen in many touches. She had obviously given access to this museum to people from many countries, including the USSR, and it was clear that since the time of that famous letter to Stalin she had not given up promoting the cause of Mayakovsky. Perhaps it was not absolutely necessary to go and hear her stories or use her library to write about Mayakovsky and the Futurists; but it is also clear that doing so could be of great help. She, like other widows, including her good friend and close neighbor in Peredelkino, Tamara Ivanova, no matter how essentially official they had been during most of their lives, was willing on occasion to go beyond official channels to extend the reputation of "her" writer. Lily had had the power of Stalin to help her with Mayakovsky, and there is no doubt that much of the poet's worldwide fame was built on that power. But even when that was gone, Lily remained a person committed to keeping Mayakovsky alive for succeeding generations. While there is no comparison between her and Nadezhda Mandelstam, she also made use of both official and unofficial channels to publish bits of Russian literary history which would remain unknown without her.

1984

Tamara Ivanova

Since Lily Brik and Tamara Ivanova were the most "official" widows we knew and were good friends of similar years and views and even shared a Peredelkino dacha together a few doors from the Pasternaks, it is appropriate to write here about the remarkable Tamara Vladimirovna Ivanova (born 1900), the widow of the one "Siberian" Serapion Brother, Vsevolod Ivanov. Ivanov was another of those who survived both an "unhealthy" association with the Serapions as well as the individualistic style of his Civil War stories of the early and mid-twenties. He survived by adapting to the new social order and rewriting his stories, and turned into a more or less acceptable Soviet classic. The early versions of a number of his stories are now difficult to find even in libraries, but his corrected collected works have been printed more than once. However, he was by no means as favored as Fedin or Leonov. Like so many others, he found himself writing some things which could not be published in Stalin's era or decades after, notably the two novels *U* and *The Uzhginsky Kremlin.*

We only met Tamara Vladimirovna a couple of times, once in the pleasant family surroundings of her large apartment in town, and once at the dacha in Peredelkino. We quickly discovered that she basically had adopted the common strategy of working, no matter how long the wait, for publication of Ivanov's works, including the unknown novels, inside the Soviet Union. This fit in perfectly with her long-held leftist views both in politics and art; in spite of being thrown out of the Party in 1919 for her bourgeois background, she had long voiced her orthodox positions and in her memoirs notes that she moved away from these "very slowly." She had little interest therefore in publishing these things abroad first; the huge Soviet audience is what she was after. On the other hand, anything we could do to propagandize Ivanov's works abroad would be good. To that end she supplied us with a number of photographs, and discussed with me the various editions of his works which had appeared in the USSR, pointing out which ones should or should not be used (because of the censored texts) for any translations we might do.

We had already shown our interest in Ivanov by publishing a translation of the original version of his most famous tale, *Armored-Train 14-69* in the second issue of *Russian Literature Triquarterly* in 1972. Essentially, however, she wanted this to be on the up-and-up, and there was no chance yet of getting any major work for translation which had not yet appeared there. It is interesting that this was her point of view even though the novel *Kremlin* had already been completely typeset for the journal *Prostor* in 1972, complete with a preface by Konstantin Fedin (an old and powerful friend), when at the last minute some overzealous flunkies from above (apparently in the directorate of the Union of Writers), stepped in and forbade the printing of the novel. The entire issue of the journal was pulped. This frustrated her, but she was still confident that time was on her side—and she was more or less correct, because after about eight more years the novel was finally published. Her incredible patience is one of her strongest characteristics. Moreover, the many deletions made by the censors were minor in relation to the whole text.

Tamara Vladimirovna was always just that—"Tamara Vladimirovna," never "Lily" or "Nadezhda" in our minds. She was a large, attractive, vital woman, used to being in charge. She had a regal air about her, the look of a lioness, perhaps an air left over from her days as a theater actress in the twenties, and the attitude of doing us a favor (which was true). We noticed that she was warm with her children, but somewhat domineering.

Like Lily, Tamara Vladimirovna lived well, and had been comfortable much of her life (her father was a store-owner and she lost at least one job in the post-revolutionary era for being "ex-bourgeois"). She was the sole and legal heir of an accepted writer to whom she had been married for 36 years. So, like Lily, she had not only the books to show the Ivanov researcher, but also a large archive of papers, particularly letters, going back to the 1920s. We were not privy to this, but judging by the samples we have in hand, there is no doubt that it was substantial. And it was well cared for, if for no other reason than the fact that her son was "Koma" (V. V.) Ivanov, generally recognized as one of the U.S.S.R.'s greatest philologists, author of many works in a variety of fields, published and known in the West as well as the U.S.S.R. This was not the kind of family where literary papers got misplaced. "Komina mama" (Koma's mother) as she was often called, with a sense of deference, would see to that even if Koma and the others did not. She, too, recognized the real nature of the Soviet regime, but she thought she would work within the system rather than against it. The exception I will discuss in a moment.

First, I must tell the most unexpected thing that we learned during our very first encounter with Tamara Vladimirovna, which reminded us in some way of the Mayakovsky's daughter theme. A chubby young boy sitting at the table with us was identified (in a whisper) as Isaac Babel's grandson. The boy had apparently just found this out himself recently. Tamara Vladimirovna had been Babel's lover in the mid-twenties, and he had, as it were, left her to the care of Ivanov when she was already pregnant. Babel was in something of a womanizer's bind, because he had sent his legal wife abroad in 1925; he travelled back and forth and conceivably could have decided to stay abroad had he wanted to (his plans are a subject of violent disagreement). He got the French branch pregnant in 1928, complicating matters. Meantime in Moscow there was the very attractive actress Tamara. (And ahead there was his last wife, Pirozhkova, and his last child, born in the 1930s.) In short, the first child Tamara had after her marriage to Ivanov was Babel's child, a fact which remained secret in most quarters for a long time, and in the West, I assume, until now.

Babel carried on an extensive correspondence with Tamara; if I recall properly, she said there were some two hundred letters, which she had in a box, and which she said no one would read until she died, at which time they would go into the official Soviet archives. (Since the important part of the Babel archive was arrested along with him in 1939 and has never come to light since then, this struck us as a bad idea, unless copies were made and put in safe places.) Since so little is known for sure about Babel in the 1925-39 period, this made the mouths of literary scholars water—but we were never to be satisfied. However, later on we did learn that she had in fact allowed the letters to be read. And those who read them—Lev and Raya Kopelev—said they were absolutely flabbergasted. Not only was there no sign of love anywhere in the letters, but barely signs of simple respect. Most were about chores which Babel wanted her to do for him, matters of money, contracts, etc. Nowhere, they said in 1983, was there a hint that these were the letters of a creative person; they were from start to finish the letters of a literary operator. Both were astonished that she had even kept the letters, let alone allowed them to be read by third parties. In response to her question of what they thought, they asked how it was she dared to keep the letters of an "enemy of the people" who had been executed. She answered, reasonably from one point of view, that Babel had never really done anything, that the charges were ridiculous, and that the correspondence in any event contained nothing in itself which was in the slightest dangerous or actionable.

Now we come to the final episode. First it is worth noting that one unpublished Ivanov novel, *U,* did make its way into samizdat and did get published abroad (by L'Age d'Homme in 1982). Whether this was a fluke or Tamara Vladimirovna actually handed the manuscript to a foreign scholar with the intent of having it studied or even published, we cannot say with assurance, although at least one copy of the manuscript was in the hands of an American scholar whom we had provided with Tamara Vladimirovna's address and instructions on how to meet her. Tamara Vladimirovna's memoirs, started as early as 1963, are about to come out in the Soviet Union. [They have since been published, with cuts and without the Kataev section. E.P.]

She did not have an independent intellect, she was not like Nadezhda Mandelstam. The main memoirs are about Fedin, Kataev, and Pasternak. Only the first of the three has any chance of appearing in uncensored form in the volume of memoirs by Tamara Vladimirovna announced to appear in 1984. Like many others, Tamara Vladimirovna was enraged by Kataev's "novelistic" memoirs, which appeared in the late seventies, *My Diamond Crown,* in which he manages to make himself look good at the expense of nearly everyone else, particularly the dead. By calling them fictionalized, but still making all his "characters'" nicknames utterly transparent, he tried to avoid the charge of inaccuracy or slander. Nevertheless, he made dozens of enemies, and Tamara Vladimirovna was one of them. Her published memoirs will not include her wonderful diatribe against Kataev entitled "I Cannot Be Silent." In the summer of 1979 she decided firmly to have her "unpublishable" memoirs printed abroad. This was a big step for someone whose point of view was generally so orthodox. She prepared the manuscript and a signed handwritten letter of explanation to go along with it. Ardis received a copy of these materials around 1980, although we do not know from whom, and she never acknowledged sending them herself. What the explanation is we do not know. It was not the first time we had witnessed difficult and repeated changes of mind.

Tamara Vladimirovna's published memoirs will no doubt include her unexpected defense of Fedin. He was a friend of Ivanov's from the first Serapion days in 1921, and he always remembered that time with fondness. As neighbors in Peredelkino, the Ivanovs and Fedin remained friends all through their lives. Most of the world knows Fedin as the head of the Writers' Union who did in his friend and neighbor Pasternak, leading the battle for his ejection from the Union, and who later did the same to Solzhenitsyn. Tamara Vladimirovna argues that Fedin was constitutionally incapable of breaking his word, and that he was caught in a hopeless struggle between friendship and duty in the Pasternak case. He had given his word to the side of duty, and he could not allow friendship to be interjected. She ignores the Solzhenitsyn episode totally.

The two parts of Tamara Vladimirovna's memoirs which can be printed only abroad relate to Kataev's *My Diamond Crown* and not only the Pasternak affair, but the whole friendship between Pasternak and Ivanov. In the Kataev blast she accuses him of lying from start to finish, of presenting such people as Khlebnikov as his acquaintance when in fact he had never even met him, of lying in ridiculous ways about people, notably another Serapion Brother who remained friends with the Ivanovs until his death, Mikhail Zoshchenko. From Mandelstam to Mayakovsky she defends others, noting that even when Russian writers were a small family in the thirties, Kataev was almost never part of their company, or invited to their readings. His disgusting role in the Pasternak attack is well known, and Tamara Vladimirovna adds details about how Pasternak refused to shake his hand. A curious aside: Kornei Chukovsky, who persistently played the role of Pasternak's friend, according to Tamara Vladimirovna came to Ivanov on one of the crucial *Zhivago* days and agreed they all had to join together in a public denunciation of Pasternak!

Tamara Vladimirovna's memoirs of Pasternak cover the whole period from 1928 to his death, but especially the long period when they were neighbors in Peredelkino (after Pasternak was given Malyshkin's dacha). She has interesting details to add about Pasternak's wartime experiences and views, including his strong disapproval of the immorality of A. N. Tolstoi, Ehrenburg, and Marshak. The Ivanovs were among those few who heard readings of chapters of *Doctor Zhivago* as they came from the typewriter, starting in 1952 apparently. In the summer of 1956 Ivanov offered to edit the novel to make it "passable"(*prokhodimyi*), and Pasternak gave him "carte blanche." She presents evidence that Pasternak did not break off relations with Fedin, despite the famous letter of 1956, and says that even after this they had hope that in some form *Doctor Zhivago* would be published, quite possibly in *Literary Moscow.*

The censored parts of Ivanova's memoirs will be published by Ardis. Once more the whole truth will be out, and the widow will have had the last word. This was probably not quite the strategy that Tamara Vladimirovna planned, but it shows once again that it is very hard to keep those close to Russian writers from collecting their memoirs, making their museums, and then—in the end—having it all see the light of day. A memoirist tends to want his work to come out. No doubt the authorities decided to let her tell how wonderful Fedin was, but persuaded her that Kataev couldn't be offended openly in a Soviet publication—nor could the whole story of the Pasternak scandal be told to the world—and after all, she was a good Soviet wife, mother and grandmother. Unfortunately for the Soviet literary establishment, they have been so malevolent over the decades that even women like Tamara Vladimirovna, who started out—and for a long time remained—staunch defenders of the new life, eventually reached the time when they could no longer repress the truth. Tamara Vladimirovna was almost eighty when Kataev's book served as the last straw. Once more the force of the widows of Russia was revealed.

1984

Literary Journalism

In the Shadow
of the
Monolith

The Russian literary scene is bizarre. The funniest new satirical work by a Soviet writer is Vladimir Voinovich's story of his own real-life battle to get into a two-room apartment which is coveted by another "writer" (only publication: *Taiwan Belongs to China*) who wants the extra square meters for a toilet (an American toilet at that) which he purchased while at the U.N. The finest novel in the last twenty years (Sokolov's *A School for Fools*) is by a Russian born in Ottawa who left Moscow this fall to become a gardener and lumberjack in the Vienna Woods. Solzhenitsyn has written a book about Lenin that his friends say is too *auto*biographical. The best-selling Soviet poet is a blind man who writes like Rod McKuen. The best Russian-language literary journal is published in Munich; the best Russian poet lives in Ann Arbor; and the first Agatha Christie in Russian has gone on sale in Jerusalem.

Because of this odd literary diaspora, a trip from Petersburg to Moscow provides only part of what one needs to know for a full picture of the current literary scene. But nearly every winter for seven years I have made the journey, and did so again in November 1975. Since these visits began in 1969, the community of Soviet writers has gone through several stages. From 1969 through 1971 there was still hope that things could be improved gradually. Then most people thought that the process of de-Stalinization, while it might have its detours and dead ends, could not be totally reversed—and that every year would see the publication of poetry and prose which couldn't have appeared the year before. Beginning in 1972, however, particularly after Nixon's visit and the internal crackdown which accompanied detente, the major topic of discussion in many families was whether to stay or to emigrate. By the end of 1975 many of the literary intellectuals who wanted to emigrate had managed to do so; those who remained had made a conscious decision to stay, either because of principles or for practical reasons.

Things (including editors and censors) are getting tougher. Voinovich and others say that the level of the literary journals is perhaps lower now than under Stalin. The mood of the liberal intelligentsia seems demoralized and apprehensive. In spite of this, writers keep writing in the face of bureaucratic meddling and foreign indifference.

Leningrad is a colder, more imperious city than Moscow. Literary trials are more frequent there—just last year Vladimir Maramzin was on his way to the Archipelago and now, thanks to a humane solution, he is in Paris, working for the new magazine, *Continent*; the sense of community there among the writers is much weaker than in Moscow. Leningrad is a city for individualists, like Nabokov. And it has been affected more by the desolation caused by the exodus than Moscow—a few good people leave, and those who remain are even more isolated. Moreover, people seem less well informed about what is happening in Russian letters abroad. For example, not all the issues of *Continent* had penetrated there during my visit, and Solzhenitsyn's *Lenin in Zurich* was not yet circulating—whereas these were available in Moscow before they were in the United States. Of course, talented writers remain, among them the poets Boris Slutsky and Viktor Sosnora, and the prose writer Andrei Bitov, all of whom have some international recognition. Joseph Brodsky's absence is felt acutely, and his new "Sonnets to Mary Stuart" are being read with special excitement.

Moscow is busier and noisier, even when the snow covers everything. There is one very mundane reason for its stronger sense of community: some years ago a special block of coop apartment buildings was built on Red Army Street near the Dynamo Stadium and the Aeroport subway. The area is now known as "Aeroport." Hundreds of writers, critics, translators, scholars—and others of less obvious direct connection to the writer's world—live there. Aeroport even has its own live-in KGB agent—General Viktor Nikolaevich Ilin, whose sphere is the Union of Writers. He has a generally good reputation even among what Westerners usually oversimplify as dissident writers. It is said that he can be tough and uncompromising, but that he can also be understanding, helpful, doesn't break his word, and has a strong sentimental streak—he is often seen patting the heads of writers' children. In fact, he has known some of the younger published writers since they were schoolchildren themselves.

Aeroport living arrangements make life rather incestuous, with frequent sexual and intellectual shifts and quakes. The writers see each other regularly, if only when small groups collect in the courtyards for "Russian conversations." The company they keep tends to be that of their peers—and perhaps in a certain sense they are cut off from "real life." When they aren't at home, they are often in "Houses of Creation" in Peredelkino and other retreats around the country—again with the same people. The Union of Writers sends them off on *komandirovki* ("business trips," with the emphasis on the root "command") during which they collect material for stories, sketches, poems, etc. Perhaps this is one reason why a popular genre is the story about an incident on a train. Currently the most visited place is called BAM (Baikal-Amur Mainline), a huge industrial complex including ports and resorts, now under construction but already much written about. Red Square demonstrations on TV are punctuated by the rising melodic line of "BAM, BAM, BAM, BAM, BAM" sung by an enthusiastic pop singer. Nothing is more salable than a BAM poem or a BAM story.

For most of the writers who remain part of the literary establishment, life goes on in its usual way. For example, every Soviet man and wife have a legal right to eighteen square meters of living space, but mere membership in the Union of Writers entitles one to an additional twenty square meters. There are special resorts, special doctors, special movies, and the luxury of the Central House of Writers in Moscow, where a gala celebration recently took place on November 7 (the anniversary of the October Revolution). Three large halls were filled with tables loaded with caviar, sturgeon, vodka, and champagne. In the inner chamber, formerly part of the Masonic Lodge which Pierre Bezukhov joined in *War and Peace,* a rock band was perched on an ornately carved wooden balcony, playing for an extremely well-dressed crowd. This is the Soviet equivalent of Hollywood stardom, and no doubt it is something for which many writers work with zeal.

I went to this gala directly from the small two-room apartment of Nadezhda Mandelstam. The storm over her memoirs has died down considerably, but there are still many who will not go to visit her, and she lives for the most part in isolation. Her opinion of contemporary literature is as harsh as it is terse ("*What* literary scene?"), and if one looks only at the Soviet equivalent of the best-seller list, one can see why.

The most famous and widely read living poet of the country is Eduard Asadov, whose works are bought by hundreds of thousands of ordinary readers. Like Rod McKuen he is an unabashed sentimentalist, but he is also a Soviet Victorian, giving such advice as don't go to bed with anyone before you sign up at the Palace of Weddings. Lumbering war novels are also read eagerly (a favorite topic of Soviet writers), and spy stories in which the KGB or its ancestors defend the fatherland are popular. But the best-selling prose work of last year was a non-fiction study by Vladimir Soloukhin, short-story writer, poet, and collector of Russian antiquities. His *The Sentence* (first published in the magazine *Moscow*) was one of the few genuine (not officially promoted) best-sellers in the Soviet Union. It tells the true story of his being diagnosed as a cancer case—and after treatment and torment discovering that the diagnosis was wrong. The abundance of personal and physiological detail, as well as the expose of some doctors, is unusual for Soviet letters.

The late Vasily Shukshin, short-story writer, movie director, and actor, has become fantastically popular. He died of a heart attack in 1974, but since then his work has been the rage of the country— particularly his story, later made into a hit movie, *The Red Snowball-Tree,* a tragedy set partly among Russian thieves and low-lifes, which played in fifty Moscow movie houses simultaneously in 1974. People from all over Russia make pilgrimages to his grave, particularly women, but he also has admirers among excellent literary critics such as Lev Anninsky; and some writers, including Solzhenitsyn, rate him highly.

Nearly everyone agrees that the Seventies are a time of prose, not poetry. The stars of the late Fifties and early Sixties are not much in evidence, though perhaps this is not their fault. Yevtushenko's reputation is lower than ever, partly because of his reputed friendship with the heads of the KGB, and while it is impossible to know the truth of this rumor, he is felt to be seriously compromised. Voznesensky has been rather silent, and not much is said about him. No one mentions Yury Kazakov or Yury Nagibin, two of the most popular prose writers of the 1960s. Akhmadulina published a book in 1975, but it contained only a handful of new poems. Aksyonov has been writing a great deal, but publishing very little. He gave lectures at UCLA last summer, with great success—an unprecedented event for a good Soviet writer, and a hopeful sign that the Union of Writers may be willing to join the real world (the poet Evgeny Vinokurov recently visited the University of Kansas and there is some hope that Akhmadulina will be allowed to visit the United States this year).

Among literary people the most highly regarded prose writers who still live and publish in the Soviet Union are Aksyonov, Trifonov, Iskander, Belov, and Aitmatov. Aitmatov is extremely popular. *The Ascent of Mount Fuji*, which he co-authored, was translated (poorly) into English last year, mainly because of its political interest (a parallel with the Solzhenitsyn case); but in his generally uncontroversial fiction there is a very heavy streak of sentimentality. Belov represents "country prose," a strain which became fashionable during the Sixties.

I saw a private showing of a marvelous West German TV documentary about this movement, with beautiful photography of the far north, where Belov lives, and an interview with him and Astafiev. They maintain, with some cogency, that the purest Russian was preserved only in the country and especially in the north—and that one cannot write good prose by living in Moscow or other cities. This has some truth to it, but if Belov's work were not enlivened by his skillful storytelling and interesting characters, his folk rusticity might seem a kind of reverse snobbery. A similar linguistic Slavophilism is found in Solzhenitsyn, who highly praises the country writers. But some critics see country prose reaching a dead end of monotony now: and indeed you can go only so far with stories of kind country folk and eccentric woodland loners.

Yury Trifonov began his career as an admirer of Hemingway and was the youngest writer to win the Stalin prize. His work has since developed considerably, and he has become, in the last few years, the chronicler of the mores and morals of the new Russian professional class: teachers, translators, office workers, managers, scholars. He does this with considerable honesty and psychological acuity, notably in a series of long stories published in *Novy mir*. One hears it said that he is able to publish grittier, more honest prose than others precisely because he is a Stalin Prize laureate. In Trifonov's world, as for example in his most recent story "Another Life" (*Novy mir*, August 1975), people live with wives and husbands they no longer love, in-laws cause daily misery, children leave the nest, and death or sickness haunts the characters, who have often failed to find the peace they seek in life. Trifonov's novel *Impatience*, about a group of nineteenth-century terrorists, has just been translated into German.

Fazil Iskander is an Abkhazian (from a small republic on the Black Sea), but writes in Russian. *The Goatibex Constellation* was his best-known longer work until a new novel, *Sandro of Chegem,* was serialized in *Novy mir* in late 1973. However, some 80 percent of the novel, including the parts mocking Stalin, was left on the floors of the editorial and censorship offices, a blow from which Iskander is still trying to recover. A satirist with large sympathies for his subjects, Iskander is in many ways the most translatable and transportable of Soviet writers, in spite of his provincial subject matter. Many of his relaxed and charming first-person narratives start with crazy incidents among southern mountain folk or collective farmers, where a goat can be worked up into a yarn.

Only a small group of Moscow writers have openly defied the authorities by publishing their works in Russian abroad. There are several centers for publishing such work in the West. Old emigres who sometimes regard the Third Wave of emigres as coddled (by their hosts), spoiled by Soviet education, and lacking in initiative, point out that no major new publishing houses have been started by the new emigres. But there were already three established ones: (1) YMCA Press in Paris, the oldest and largest (about twelve titles per year), Solzhenitsyn's current publisher, but specialists in theology and philosophy; (2) Possev, in Munich, a somewhat more militant and political house; (3) Ardis in Ann Arbor, for unpublished classics and for younger writers. There are also two "thick" journals (a Russian tradition for 175 years), combining literature, history and politics—*The New Review (Novy zhurnal)* in New York and *Facets (Grani)* in Munich. The quality of these journals, and of the main Russian-language newspaper, Paris's *Russian Thought,* has not been high in recent years, but it has been improved by the Third Wave.

The most interesting new Russian-language periodical was founded with the help of Solzhenitsyn and Ullstein Verlag, and is named, for reasons which must be obvious, *Continent,* with a subtitle, in bold type, "A Literary, Socio-political, and Religious Journal." It is published in Russian and plans are being made for translations into other major languages (the first selection in English will soon appear). It is edited in Paris by Vladimir Maximov, author of *Seven Days of Creation,* who emigrated from the USSR two years ago after being thrown out of the Union of Writers for excessive candor. It was hoped that this new journal would be the great tribune of the Third Wave—it could be the liberated voice—and that its quality would be high. Moreover, *Continent* is unique in openly publishing some writers—such as Voinovich and Vladimir Kornilov—who still live in Moscow. It is printed in a small four-and-a-half by seven inch format so that it can be easily held in the hand, or hidden in the pocket. Of course, it is not allowed through Soviet customs, but nevertheless copies get into the Soviet Union, and anyone in Moscow who is diligent can find all of the first five issues.

Continent's editorial board includes Andrei Sakharov, Galich (the well-known poet and chansonnier whose songs many Russian intellectuals know by heart), Ionesco, Milovan Djilas, Robert Conquest, John Bayley and others, including Naum Korzhavin, a talented poet in his fifties; though little published in Moscow, he is about to publish two books and has written fascinating essays analyzing the Russian intelligentsia. Andrei Sinyavsky (Abram Tertz) was on the board through the first four issues, but he resigned in an argument over his wife's role in the journal before No. 5 appeared. He continues to lecture at the Sorbonne. The opening issue of *Continent* showed promise, but most readers agreed that its quality declined in the subsequent three issues—only to rise again, rather dramatically, in No. 5. It has published poems by Brodsky, Galich, and Korzhavin; Tertz-Sinyavsky's long essay "The Literary Process in Russia"; Solzhenitsyn's "An Unpublished Chapter from *The First Circle*"; Maramzin's "The Story of the Marriage of Ivan Petrovich"; Viktor Nekrasov's charming "Notes of a Loafer"; Voinovich's "Incident in the Metropole"; and Kornilov's "Without Arms, Without Legs."

Probably the most important prose in *Continent* is the series of excerpts from Vasily Grossman's *For the Right Cause*. But the late Grossman's friends in the Soviet Union are angry with the editors for printing only parts of a novel which is famous for being the only manuscript in the history of Russian literature to have been put under physical arrest. After Grossman sent it to a Soviet journal, the editor passed on the offending pages to the KGB, who sent operatives with a warrant for the arrest of the manuscript. All known copies, drafts, and notes were carried off, and, so everyone thought, destroyed. Then, mysteriously, some years later a copy turned up, and then multiplied.

Translations traditionally form an important part of Russian "thick" journals. So far *Continent* has published translations of Cardinal Mindszenty's memoirs, works by Ionesco and Djilas, and most recently, Koestler's *Darkness at Noon*—a sensation for a Russian audience, and one of the main reasons why No. 5 has been praised so highly. The journal averages 450 pages per issue, about half of which is literary. The editors have obviously been pushed into printing some things they will later regret: the terrible poems of "Wanderer" (pseudonym of the archbishop of San Francisco, whose sister is editor-in-chief of *Russian Thought* in Paris and, like her brother, on the editorial board of *Continent*), prose by Sinyavsky's wife Maria Rozanova, and a boring story by Iosif Bogoraz ("The Stoolie"). Nevertheless, *Continent* has obviously become a major force in Russian letters right now. It deserves praise and support—and along with the works of Solzhenitsyn it is among the most frequent topics of discussion among Moscow and Leningrad intellectuals.

What are the Russians talking most about now? The furor over Mme Mandelstam's *Hope Abandoned* has given way to vitriolic arguments about Solzhenitsyn's *The Oak and the Calf*. *The Oak* is the story of Solzhenitsyn's literary career from its public beginning in 1961, when, as he relates, his friend Lev Kopelev took the manuscript of *SH-854* (later censored down to *One Day of Ivan Denisovich*) to *Novy mir,* until his exile from the USSR. The 620 pages of this sprawling, often sloppily written book are highly readable. The major figure, apart from the author, is Alexander Tvardovsky, the editor of *Novy mir* who first published Solzhenitsyn, and who then alternately sponsored him, placated him, put him off, and defended him over the years until Tvardovsky was forced to retire from the journal (he died not long after in December 1971).

Nothing is more hotly argued now than Solzhenitsyn's portrait of Tvardovsky. Depending on whom you talk to, Solzhenitsyn's picture of Tvardovsky is unwittingly or wittingly vicious; disrespectful or respectful; tendentious or tender; mendacious or objective. Most of the former editorial board of *Novy mir* are up in arms (for themselves as well as Tvardovsky); Roy Medvedev has condemned Solzhenitsyn's portrait in a long rebuttal. While Solzhenitsyn seems not to be the most objective man in the world, the vehemence and variety of the reaction make me think (especially after the Mandelstam affair) that *on the whole* Solzhenitsyn comes close to the truth. The hostility of some criticism springs primarily from the Russian tendency to prefer saints' lives to candid biography. They want to remember Tvardovsky only as the brilliant author of the World War II poem *Tyorkin,* fighter for truth and justice, and not as a man sometimes debilitated by alcoholism and long membership in the club of "bosses," as the Russians term higher-ups.

Speaking of saints, Solzhenitsyn's most recent book in Russian, *Lenin in Zurich,* is being read with more humor and less pleasure. It contains an omitted chapter from the first "Bundle" or "Fascicle" (as Solzhenitsyn calls the parts of his World War I novel), plus ten chapters taken from Fascicles II and III (*October 1916, March 1917*). Solzhenitsyn had written part of this before he left Russia. When he found himself in Zurich he did some further research and decided to print these motley chapters together in advance of the entire novel. This was obviously done for polemical purposes—another blow against the Soviets. But the sad result is a kind of inverse *biographie romancée,* complete with psychological eavesdropping on Lenin's inner thoughts, as for example when he is seen standing alone, staring out over a rippling lake and pondering revolutionary tactics and a *ménage à trois* with Krupskaya and the disturbing, delectable Inessa.

This is funny enough, but the peculiar thing is that the portrait of Lenin is being called a self-portrait of the author. A man who knew Solzhenitsyn for many years insisted to me that Solzhenitsyn has not only given Lenin his own language and traits of character, but that he has even made him relive certain incidents from his own life. It is certainly true that reading *Lenin in Zurich* and *The Calf Butts the Oak* together one is struck by the similar, almost stream-of-consciousness, style, and by the obvious parallels between Lenin plotting revolutionary "blows" against the tsarist regime and Solzhenitsyn later preparing his attack against the Soviet system. One could deduce that Solzhenitsyn feels great kinship with Lenin.

The attitude toward Solzhenitsyn's *GULAG,* at least in liberal circles, is totally different. Russians find these volumes devastating. Still, opinions of Solzhenitsyn as a writer in the Soviet Union vary greatly: a few consider him a great writer, an equal of Tolstoy; most draw a distinction between his political greatness and his artistic abilities; many agree that he cannot handle the novel form, particularly when he gets away from his primary subject, the prison camp. I would say that Solzhenitsyn is the poet of scorn, and by itself that is probably not enough for art. But the heavy irony and sledge-hammer blows which can ruin his fiction enable him to deliver his relentless attack on the Soviet system, and no one doubts his pre-eminence as historian and poet of the Archipelago.

Solzhenitsyn's old prison mate and friend Lev Kopelev published in 1975 his remarkable 700-page memoir *To Be Preserved Forever*—the motto on the dossiers of political prisoners. (It is being translated into ten languages.) Kopelev also tells a story of war and the camps, but from a quite different point of view. Kopelev was a true believer from youth, and even in prison he wrote poems of praise to Stalin. He has greater knowledge of and sympathy for the Party faithful than Solzhenitsyn, and one learns more from Kopelev about how they really think and live. He was arrested in 1945 for "bourgeois humanism"—i.e., trying to prevent atrocities against German civilians—and his memoir is in part the story of his own very gradual disillusionment with the system.

The implications of Soviet membership in the Universal Copyright Convention are being discussed with great urgency. To help implement copyright control and sales abroad, the Soviet government has set up VAAP, and every contract signed by a Soviet writer now is accompanied by a release form in which the writer makes VAAP his agent for dealing with foreign rights. Without the help and approval of VAAP, nothing written and published after May 1973 in the USSR can be published abroad. Moreover, it is rumored that laws have been passed making it illegal for Soviet writers to publish their work abroad first. This belief was strengthened by what some took as a threat from a VAAP officer, Boris Pankin, in the *Literary Gazette* some time ago.

Those who have published abroad openly, and those who are considering doing so, are in a quandary, and the emigre publishing houses are holding files full of works until the writers decide whether to go ahead. They can't predict what the official reaction is going to be, and there have been no test cases so far. To add to the difficulty, all works published in the USSR are censored and edited—and some writers would prefer to see their complete versions published, even if in a foreign language. It remains to be seen whether VAAP will permit this.

Voinovich, one of the most popular new writers of the Sixties, is perhaps the most interesting case. He was thrown out of the Union of Writers two years ago, after he wrote an open letter criticizing Boris Pankin for hinting that writers publishing abroad could be punished. Voinovich is now unable to publish in the USSR, but he behaves almost as if he were a free man. He has published in *Continent;* the first two parts of his novel (written between 1963 and 1970) *The Life and Extraordinary Adventures of Private Ivan Chonkin* just came out

(YMCA Press, 1975), and his satire *Ivankiada* is being published in the United States.

Chonkin may turn out to be among the most popular Russian works published abroad in recent years (it will be published in the US by Farrar, Straus and Giroux). Voinovich has handled all of these publications rather openly, through a lawyer in Seattle. And while communications with him are still often carried on by hand, through friends, Voinovich is willing to discuss his situation on the international telephone. Talking to him, I understood that he was simply tired of being afraid and of giving in. Now he is calm and resigned, he says, to anything that may happen—arrest, exile, or even death—whatever will be.

His satire *Ivankiada* is the account of how he got his apartment in the writers' co-op—after monumental and petty obstacles were put in his way by a well-connected Party functionary who wanted to get the extra apartment next to his own, tear down a wall, and install an American toilet. This sounds trivial, but what is original is the way Voinovich describes all of the steps, the meetings of the co-op boards, angry and fearful conversations with all kinds of Soviet people, and the names and offices of the bigwigs involved (including some of the most important men in Moscow). Russian readers say that Voinovich's document provides a microcosmic view of how everyday Soviet life works.

Chonkin, which was repeatedly rejected by Soviet publishers and attacked by colleagues in the Union of Writers, is the story of a bumbling Soviet Schweik during the beginning of World War II. Its satire is mild, but in the Soviet Union the Soviet Army is one thing you don't criticize. It is a very readable and funny novel, with interesting portrayals of country life and psychology. There is even some mild sexual detail, and language which does not meet Soviet standards of purity. Both will seem rather tame to a Westerner, but the book is enjoyable in a way that is very unusual for Russian writing—relaxed and good-humored, with no "cursed questions," no soap-box rhetoric.

I think one recent event will leave a mark on the literature of this decade. This is the debut of Sasha Sokolov, a thirty-one-year-old Muscovite whose first novel, *A School for Fools,* is being published abroad in Russian this month, with English and German translations underway. While it is not an anti-Soviet book or a political one, both its subject and its form make *A School for Fools* censorable in the USSR, and so Sokolov sent it abroad anonymously. Joseph Brodsky originally picked it out of a pile of *samizdat* manuscripts, and during the last year this "enchanting text," as Wladimir Weidle, the most distinguished Russian critic living abroad, calls it, has created a stir among advance readers. Vladimir Markov says there has never been anything like it in Russian literature, "though if Joyce had written the last chapter of *Ulysses* in Russian it would have sounded like this."

A School for Fools describes life in the country, centering on a "special" school for retarded, and often psychotic, children. The novel's nameless hero, and one of the main narrators, is a former pupil in the special school. His father is a chief prosecutor, responsible among other things for the schizophrenia of his only son. The student's only hero is the eloquent geographer Norvegov, an idealist and dreamer who hates the way the school and the society are run. His speeches, along with the young man's hallucinatory reminiscences, are among the best parts of the novel, whose characters include the narrator's mistress, some whimsical railroad workers, and some semi-mythic people whose existence remains in doubt. Sokolov is very Russian in his moral concerns, particularly in showing with imaginative force the past causes and future consequences of a given act. But in his sense of measure, his quiet wit, and his delicacy of touch he is rather un-Russian.

After Sokolov wrote this book he fell in love with a young Austrian woman, and when she was barred from the USSR he publicly protested. His marriage to a foreigner was opposed by his father—a retired two-star general in the GRU (Soviet military intelligence)—and at a news conference Sokolov accused his father of spying on the United States and Canada when he was with the Soviet embassy in Ottawa during the war. His father responded by proclaiming him mad. The story has many ups and downs from that point, but after the Helsinki pact and his fiancee's televised hunger strike in a Viennese church, Sokolov was given an exit visa. He is now working in the Vienna Woods.

In contrast to Sokolov, writers over forty, whether they live in the USSR or abroad, and whether they publish in *Novy mir* or in *Continent,* tend to be "realists," conservatives in form. It is impossible to tell the dissidents from the socialist realists. Trifonov, Iskander, Voinovich, Nekrasov, Solzhenitsyn—they are all men of the old school, in the grand tradition of Tolstoyan prose, or, less grandly, as it has passed through several decades and numerous Fadeevs. At Trifonov's apartment a photograph of Ernest Hemingway hangs on the wall; Voinovich uses a rather old-fashioned nineteenth-century narrator in *Chonkin;* and formally large parts of Solzhenitsyn's novels can be said to be pure socialist realism. Some even compare him to the grandfather of socialist realism, Chernyshevsky, arguing that he is righteous, tendentious, wooden, humorless and clumsy in romance. Indeed the Russians are generally proud of their eschewal of "modernism." One critic I talked to at length last November argued strongly that now there was "one literature," a "single flow," whether it was published abroad or at home made no difference—there was essential unity in theme and manner.

However, there are some new writers—mostly in their thirties—who, like Sokolov, are more adventurous in form. To varying degrees they show the influence of Joyce, Bely, Faulkner, and other classic twentieth-century Western writers. The short stories of Maramzin exemplify this trend. It is characteristic that *Continent* should publish one of his most conservative tales. Others contain a variety of experiments with unreliable narrators, take-offs on Nabokov, inverted structures, stream-of-consciousness dream sequences, tortured diction borrowed from the uneducated Soviet man in the street. In this Maramzin is strongly influenced by Andrei Platonov, the Thirties writer rediscovered in the 1960s, whose language frequently borders on absurdity or insanity or both.

In poetry, a somewhat similar line is being followed by Eduard Limonov, who grew up in Kharkov and now lives in New York. His work has been influenced by the absurdist school of the 1930s called the Oberiuty. More decadent, and also more fantastic, is the prose of Yury Mamleev, who has spawned a school of *samizdat* imitators, even though he has never been published in Moscow and has been living in New York. Mamleev writes about such Soviet *bizarreries* as a psychopathic vampire, a kind of bloodoholic, who is trying to stay on the wagon, or at least on the Moscow bloodmobile (he manages to refrain from killing people when he gets a job in a bloodbank). Crude scatological detail and spoofs of metaphysical fiction are also typical of Mamleev's work, some of which has recently appeared in *The New Review* in New York.

From the Soviet Union to Israel there are many young unpublished writers experimenting with everything from concrete poetry to mystical monologues, as lacking in intelligibility as in punctuation. Much of this work is sterile, but it typifies an honest effort to recover some of the avant-garde spirit of the Twenties, from which most Russians were cut off. It should be remembered that until the Sixties Russians knew virtually nothing about Kafka, Proust, Faulkner, or Camus—and Joyce has still not been published officially.

Joseph Brodsky, whose new book *A Part of Speech* will appear shortly in Russian, is more a traditionalist than an experimenter—but he has done things with rhyme, grammar, and logic that even a Futurist would flaunt. The intentional collapse of connectives in his "Sonnets to Mary Stuart" again suggests Platonov, and there are some purely cinematic effects; but the basic form and some of the motifs go back to Pushkin. *A Part of Speech* is made up exclusively of work done since Brodsky left the USSR in 1972, including a Derzhavinesque tribute to Marshal Zhukov (which annoyed many fellow emigres when it was published in *Continent*), a poem about Venice, a cycle of Mexican poems, a London poem, some love poems, and a long philosophical monologue called "Lullaby of Cape Cod." Travelogues are a weakness of all recent emigre writers, but presumably this enthusiasm for exotic place-name rhymes will pass. Brodsky is at his best in memory poems like the sonnets to Mary Stuart, or his meditations such as the "Lullaby" (he recalls being bowled over by the sound, in Russian, of the title "Lullaby of Birdland"). No book of poetry is more keenly awaited in the Soviet Union.

The hunger for books and the passionate desire to contribute to European culture continue to prevail among the intelligentsia in the Soviet Union. Western reprints of Nabokov's Russian novels and the complete poetry of Akhmatova and Mandelstam are passed around with an excitement which the blase Westerner might not at first understand. Soviet conservatives who enforce customs rules banning the import into Russia of books printed in Russian have still not discovered that such works are no more a threat to their system than *The Catcher in the Rye* was to the U.S. We can hope the "spirit of Helsinki" and detente will yet lead to more freedom, but at the moment Russians, wherever they are, have to read, write, and publish in the shadow of a monolith.

1976

A Disabled Literature:
Are There Any Writers Left
in the Soviet Union?

I.

Official Soviet Russian literature is like wheelchair basketball: one may be impressed by the vigor of the players, or the remarkable muscles developed in limited areas, and individual stars do emerge— but there is something fundamentally wrong with it. And it isn't really basketball. The Soviet writer's handicap is clear—totalitarian control in the literal meaning of the word "total." There are entire areas of human life which Soviet writers are forced to lie about, or, at very best, to ignore. For example: history, philosophy, politics, all other countries, education, industry, agriculture, religion, and sex. Writers breathe these restrictions through every pore; then they are told to write something called "socialist realism."

In practice this means an all-thumbs imitation of the Turgenev line of the nineteenth-century Russian novel in characterization and style, including obligatory nature descriptions which sound like the Woody Allen parodies in *Love and Death*. It is not easy to write a realistic novel without telling the truth, so the Soviet writer's task is unenviable. Of course, in theory it is possible for a writer of genius to take any number of restrictions, overcome them to his advantage; but in practice there are no convincing examples of this. I cannot think of a single work of merit published in the USSR which would have been written as it was if the author knew that he would not have to worry about the censors and editors who would scrutinize his work. And I am speaking of the most honest Soviet writers.

The clearest example is Vladimir Voinovich. The first volume of his novel *The Life and Adventures of Private Ivan Chonkin* was written in the belief that it would somehow get published in the Soviet Union (it didn't, and turned out to be one of the major factors in removing Voinovich from Soviet libraries and life); the second

112

volume, written when he knew it would be published only abroad, is markedly different, sharper in its satire, more vehement in its anger. The first volume was honest in most ways, but the second is as different as if Voinovich had had an arrow removed from his throat. (On Christmas Day 1980, Voinovich left the USSR.)

One can follow the careers of several authors from works they knew would be published at home, to ones they were hopeful about, to ones they were dubious about, and then to works they knew were only for "free" publication. All of the stages are clearly visible as the author gradually liberates himself. Thus even in Solzhenitsyn's case one goes from a version of *One Day in the Life of Ivan Denisovich* written for a Soviet journal to his latest full version. Whether anyone can truly and completely liberate himself after 40 years in the USSR is another question, and a major one, which awaits its answer.

The interested reader, incidentally, need not take my word for all this. Soviet cultural supervisors hypocritically complain that Soviet literature is not available in the United States; but Soviet Russian literature is actually more available here than it is in the USSR, and much of it is translated by the Soviets' own English-language propaganda mill, Progress Publishers, and sold at cut-rate prices, mainly to a gullible third-world audience. Their monthly magazine *Soviet Literature* (in English and eight other languages) is readily available in this country. I recommend it as the best way to get the official Soviet Party view of Russian literature. It is what the editors (some of the most senile mossbacks in the Party apparatus) imagine is the acme of Soviet literature, but it would be hard intentionally to put together a more puerile compendium of swill. Progress also publishes a line of books, which include nineteenth-century classics, a few contemporaries worth reading (Iskander, Nagibin, Soloukhin, Shukshin), but mainly party bozos who have no hope of ever being translated by Western publishing houses. A small library of these, even making allowances for the occasionally lunatic English of the translations, will convince the reader that much Soviet literature is simple-minded, provincial, aimed essentially at children, and (aside from the politics) on the level of *Little Men* or the *Boy's Life* inspirational fiction of the 1950s.

Now let us leave aside "most" Soviet literature and concentrate on a few genuine artists. The very concept of "Soviet literature" is complicated enough to require definition. There are four kinds of Soviet *Russian* writers: (1) those who live and publish in the USSR exclusively; (2) those who live in the USSR and publish most of their work there, but some works only abroad, in Russian; (3) those who live in the USSR and publish exclusively abroad; (4) those who were born in the USSR, educated there, and spent most of their lives there, but who have emigrated in the last eight years and now publish exclusively abroad.

These writers are basically all part of the same Russian literature of the Soviet period. They share a common heritage, language, and general subject matter—i.e., life in the USSR. They read and write for one another and their Soviet audience, both the Soviet audience in the USSR and that composed of some 350,000 emigres. One should note that the official Soviet definition of "Soviet literature" is quite different: they insist that Soviet literature is "multinational" and that one who wants to discuss it must know the writings of the Azerbaijanis, Karakulalpakians, Latvians, and 50 other language groups. In fact, because of the Russians' imperial enslavement of all these other nationalities, each national literature is merely an inferior copy of the power culture's own Party literature. The best of it is translated into Russian immediately, and writers such as Aitmatov, Dumbadze, and Bykov may almost be treated as Russian writers. All are under the same central censorship and control. When squeezed firmly in interviews, they all make the same noises.

I will focus primarily on the established writers, not the new ones. While there is a degree of subjectivity in this, I think any reasonably informed person would mention Trifonov and Rasputin (category 1), Bitov and Iskander (category 2), Vladimov (category 3), Aksyonov and Voinovich (formerly of category 1, later in category 2, and then recently, in the last year or two, in category 3, and during the writing of this essay shifting into category 4). Except for Rasputin, all have lived most recently in Moscow, and they know one another reasonably well. They have shared the same language and experience, and they are Soviet in their subject matter—in spite of Iskander's and Rasputin's special settings.

Among Soviet Russian writers who have not published in Russian abroad, Yury Trifonov is certainly preeminent. To return to my opening comparison again, he is so good that one can often forget the fact that he is in that wheelchair. If one wants to know what Soviet urban life is and has been like, no Soviet writer provides a better picture than Trifonov. His prose is a solid machine moving methodically through the moral and material crises of the intelligentsia and the middle class. The stories in the trilogy *The Long Goodbye* are set in the present. His most recent, and ambitious, novels are largely historical. These include *The House on the Embankment* and what he regards as his most important work, *The Old Man.* The latter and Trifonov's posthumous novel *Time and Place* are the only major works which have not yet been translated.

And while Trifonov is an honest writer who is controversial in the USSR because of his candor and boldness, he has to leave much beneath the surface. One senses a submerged anger in Trifonov, and it is doubtful that *The House on the Embankment* would contain so much that is purely implicit if he had written it "for abroad." Indeed, non-Soviet readers will miss much that Trifonov's home readers immediately understand—because of their shared experiences with Stalin and the history of the Party leaders in that "house" (an apartment house) on the embankment. Virtually all of Trifonov's mature works already or soon will exist in translations into English, French, and German, so any reader can see for himself that Trifonov is an important contemporary European writer.

The opposition between city and country has been an important theme in Soviet writing from the start, and for the last 25 years country prose has been discussed exhaustively by Soviet critics and writers, with conclusions of all kinds (including the conclusion that it does not exist). Until his death in 1974, Shukshin was popularly regarded as the leading practitioner. Now the field belongs to such established writers as Fyodor Abramov, Viktor Astafiev, Vasily Belov, Boris Mozhaev, Vladimir Soloukhin, Vitali Syomin, and Valentin Rasputin. At their best they help revitalize the homogenized and bureaucratized literary language that central control of literature has promoted; they present unusual character types and show a small part of how rural life and agriculture have been devastated by the Soviet regime (for example, such things as pigs being fed black bread instead of grain, because it is cheaper—due to state subsidy—and more plentiful). They show traditional emotions and traditional values. These features help explain why Solzhenitsyn has repeatedly praised the country writers (though one should take Solzhenitsyn's desire to be admired for his country prose style as seriously as a Playmate wanting to be loved for her mind). At its worst, which I think is more often the case, country prose is provincial, monotonous, and sentimental. Sometimes it is nothing more than barely fictionalized ethnography, as artistic as *The Loves of the Plants* and more tedious than Gogol's *Evenings on a Farm near Dikanka.* Its interest for non-Soviet readers is mainly sociological, and this is not just because the culture is so alien. The world of Márquez is no less alien—but as he presents it, it is alive; the fullness, passion, and color of life delight us. The bovine plod of much Soviet rural prose is soporific.

The country writer who has received most attention in the past few years is Valentin Rasputin (born 1937). He is a Siberian, and his view and knowledge of the world are naturally different from what they would be if he were from the literary capitals. He has achieved a high level of honesty in describing life in his native regions; this and the fact that his prose style is rich—avoiding both the homogenized Party lingo and the extremes of dialect—make him a hope for the future. Because he is now being touted by the establishment as a success story, it will be interesting to see what happens to him. So far he has refused to do the hack work usually demanded of an officially successful career (messages to the people on Soviet holidays, etc.). It seems to me that given Rasputin's realism and honesty it will be extremely difficult for him to remain detached, and moreover as he approaches his mid-40s (traditionally the peak years for a prose writer) he may discover he has written something so truthful and so good that it will be unpublishable in his homeland. His attraction to tragedy, the irrational, and traditional human values would seem to drive him toward this point. His interest for the non-Soviet reader is somewhat questionable. His novel *Live and Remember* was published here by Macmillan without creating a stir. An even better work, *Goodbye to Matyora,* also published here, was also remaindered, showing that some good writers do not travel well.

Of all the writers in the USSR, Fazil Iskander (born 1929) is surely the one whose works can best survive translation and cultural export. One can easily imagine him becoming a best seller in this country. This is somewhat paradoxical, because, though he writes in Russian, Iskander comes from a tiny nation that few Americans have ever heard of—Abkhazia. This so-called republic lies beside Georgia on the Black Sea. As the world will discover sooner or later, Iskander is the Gabriel Garcia Márquez of Abkhazia. The major work of Iskander's life is a novel called *Sandro of Chegem*. In a series of semi-independent tales, Iskander tells the story of Uncle Sandro from the 1880s to the 1960s—and Sandro's story is also the story of the Abkhazian people, with all their customs, superstitions, passions, and sufferings. In Iskander's case regionalism is not a barrier to understanding, because there is an epic, universal quality to his writing. He is a comic writer, and certainly much of the value of *Sandro* as entertainment is due to the humor. But like many comic writers, Iskander is basically serious— even melancholic, reminiscent of Gogol. The long and wonderful section on Stalin in *Sandro* entitled "The Feast of Belshazzar," shows both Iskander's dark and light sides. The unflattering picture of a republic under Soviet domination is so violently at variance with the idealized, paternalistic Muscovite view that *Sandro*, the great work of Iskander's life (and no doubt of his people), quickly ran afoul of the censors. Roughly 20 percent of the novel was published in Moscow as if it were the whole work (1973). In 1979 a then-complete edition was published in Russian by Ardis, and in 1981 a second volume followed, making the novel almost as long as *War and Peace.*

Iskander's is an especially depressing case. He is a writer of the first rank, and he obviously has very little interest in politics as such. By no stretch of the imagination could he be called a dissident. *Sandro* was obviously a book from the heart and soul; its satire is more Horatian than Juvenalian, and only the unreasoning practices of Soviet literary superintendents kept a Soviet publishing house from having the honor of bringing out a book that would truly make the world look on with envy. In 1983-84 Random House published the English translation, complete in two volumes, to wide critical praise.

Andrei Bitov (born 1937) is also in the prime of his career. His prose style is instantly recognizable. The serpentine syntax, the complex series of subordinations, the startling but graceful use of abstractions and metaphors present a formidable challenge to the translator. For over a decade Bitov has been known at home mainly as the author of short prose pieces, and some of these, such as "A Country Place" (translated as "Life in Windy Weather") are masterful; other stories turned out to be disguised sections of a large novel—the major work of his life—which Bitov could not get printed in the USSR: *Pushkin House* (in Russian the title refers to the main literary archive in Leningrad, which houses all the papers of the classics, and also to Russia itself, Pushkin's "home").

The novel was published in Russian in the United States in 1978 to almost universal acclaim. If Hemingway was Trifonov's early influence, Bitov's masters are obviously Dostoevsky and Nabokov.

117

Among other things, they share St. Petersburg (Leningrad). Like Nabokov's *The Gift, Pushkin House* is a "museum of Russian literature." It is the story of a twentieth-century Soviet superfluous man, a "hero of his time" (the post-Stalin generation), who is playing his own version of "fathers and sons." The classic Russian novels of the last century echo on almost every page, and one can say that an important theme in *Pushkin House* is the Russian novel and its development. Bitov's deeply introspective attention to motivation puts him with Dostoevsky as a psychological novelist; and Dostoevsky's characters and character relationships are everywhere. But Dostoevsky's journalese, supernumeraries, and messy structures are foreign to Bitov. Instead we find a neatly planned modern novel with strong suggestions of Nabokov in the structural symmetries, character parallels, the use of literary allusion, fatidic numbers, intentional ambiguities, and undermining of the fictional reality by variant versions of important events. As a melding of traditional and modern elements, *Pushkin House* is a *tour de force*. It is as much Bitov's modern form and style that made the novel unpublishable at home as it was the themes—which include the sins of the fathers during Stalin's rule, the relative virtues of aristocracy and meritocracy, and alcohol as a Russian institution. But even if Bitov writes nothing else, his permanent place in Russian literature has been firmly established.

Readers of Soviet literature have been familiar with the name of Vasily Aksyonov since the early 1960s when his first stories established him as the spokesman of a new generation, the post-Stalin intelligentsia, the young liberals who helped deepen the thaw. "Halfway to the Moon" and "A Ticket to the Stars" were tremendously influential stories, and Aksyonov became the most popular Soviet prose writer. But rapid fluctuations in the political temperature were reflected in his career; his works were published, but erratically and in censored form. His efforts to expand the stylistic, structural, and thematic limits of Soviet writing presented a continual challenge to editorial and political conservatives. In 1979 Aksyonov's last major literary work was published—his translation of E. L. Doctorow's *Ragtime.* It was a sensation for the Russians, and in spite of the editor's red ink, Aksyonov managed to preserve some frank sexual descriptions. This brought down the wrath of the Party; the editor was summoned to the Central Committee with the original in one hand and

Aksyonov's version in the other. Separate book publication (it had appeared only in a journal) was forbidden.

But it was Aksyonov's role in putting together the *Metropole* anthology of prose and poetry by 23 Soviet writers that was the last straw for the authorities. After *Metropole* was rejected by the Union of Writers and then published in the West by Ardis, Aksyonov resigned from the union over the bosses' harassment of the less well-known contributors to the anthology. Led by a smooth-talking hack named Felix Kuznetsov, a campaign of threats, blackmail, and blacklisting was conducted against many of the 23 writers. Aksyonov's departure from the Soviet Union this summer was one result. He is currently lecturing at American universities. In January 1980 he was deprived of Soviet citizenship. Eventually, in 1983, Norton published the complete *Metropole* in English.

When Aksyonov's long novel *The Burn* appeared in Italian translation in early 1980, Yury Maltsev, the best-known chronicler of emigre Russian letters, wrote: "*The Burn* has created a sensation. It is a monumental work which the author labored over for six years. It is undoubtedly the high point of his career, his most profound, most mature and most brilliant work; it immediately moves Aksyonov to the front ranks of Russian literature today." Subtitled "The Late Sixties, the Early Seventies," *The Burn* is set mainly in the period from the Prague Spring to the beginning of the "Third Wave" of emigration in 1973-74. It is a social, political, and philosophical chronicle in the best traditions of Russian literature. Its subject is the destiny of Russia and the Russian people, especially the intelligentsia. In its kaleidoscope we see dozens of characters, hear hundreds of points of view, ranging from the secret police and jazz musicians to intellectuals' kitchen discussions, to those of the average Russian, the simple, crude, beaten-down, and cruel habitues of beer stands and soccer matches. The central device the author uses to take us through Russian thought and feeling in this period is the description of five heroes (a physicist, a doctor, a writer, a sculptor, and a saxophone player), all of whom have the same middle name (patronymic) and all of whom, it turns out in the end, are really parts of one character, a creative Russian (the "burn" of inspiration can be artistic or scientific) who lives through his era and tries to make sense out of Russia and its peculiar kind of totalitarianism. It is not a straightforward narrative, and as in many of Aksyonov's works there is sometimes a mixture of fantasy and reality. The narrator often calls into question the reality of events and characters he creates; the chronology is not linear; the language is rich and inventive. In these three respects Aksyonov's prose is unlike typical Soviet writing. Moreover, in sexual matters it is absolutely candid. Nor are the themes parochial. Aksyonov knows the rest of the world exists, likes it, and is not afraid to use it. His cosmopolitanism was always one of the things that the secretaries of the Union of Writers found suspicious. Good Soviet writers are self-sufficient; nothing outside the Soviet Union really has to be shown (except spies, reactionaries, and drug addicts). The condemnation of Stalin, police, executioners (real and metaphorical, including executioners of ideas), and the system itself is as profound as the author's sympathy for the Russian people. As two fine Russian emigre critics, Peter Vail and Alexander Genis, have said, *The Burn,* translated in 1984, is an encyclopedia of Soviet life. And it is an attempt to make sense of it all.

While Aksyonov has always been hard to categorize, it would seem he is now in his most productive period as a novelist, since *The Burn* was followed by another major work, *The Island of Crimea.* It was written in certainty that it would be published abroad, written at a time in Aksyonov's life when he had essentially given up hope that he could continue to be published in the USSR; and I think that it shows a certain liberation and relaxation that is not so clear in *The Burn* (also unpublished at home, but written when the future seemed more fluid and uncertain). *The Island of Crimea* is also rather more conventional than *The Burn* in form, though again we have a mixture of fantasy and realism. (The translation was published by Random House in 1983.) He has also just completed *The Paperscape* and the long novel, *Say, Cheeese,* which are scheduled for translation. Aksyonov, who has always written in many genres, became the only Soviet writer to have a major success on the stage: the French version of *The Heron* was a hit in 1983.

One of the few Soviet writers still living in the USSR in 1981, who had a national reputation before becoming known as a dissident, and who has published only abroad for many years, is Georgy Vladimov. His haunting novel *Faithful Ruslan* was published here last year in English, and received very warm reviews. Some reviewers, and even the publishers, presented it as a "dog story," but that is not really what it is. One does learn a lot about dogs, and how they are trained to guard prisoners in the Gulag; but dogs are used mainly to show the character of human beings. What we learn is how one becomes a faithful soldier, how one remains permanently attached to the service, even when circumstances change drastically. Thus Ruslan is trained, becomes the selfless servant, and remains so, even when the camp where he serves is closed down for good. Ruslan is not destroyed as he is supposed to be, but is given to the "shabby man" (a former prisoner). The man thinks the dog is a companion—but Ruslan is really still guarding him. He cannot learn anything new. He is still utterly convinced he is performing his service; he is even noble in his blind belief, and he will kill if need be to go on guarding the man as he always has. It is not hard to see this as an allegory for the Stalinists who could not (and still cannot) change, in spite of Stalin's death. The Ruslans are still there, still obedient to their old training, perhaps even decent and honorable in their own context.

Chilling as this allegory is, it alone would not have created Vladimov's reputation as a writer. The allegory aside, the story he tells is compelling. Bit by bit, Vladimov builds his world. He is a realist in the best sense of the word—he knows the world he is describing down to its finest details, and his prose is as unhackneyed as it is lucid. Actually, Vladimov's Soviet reputation was made with novels about several completely different kinds of world—the world of miners in *The Big Ore* (1961) and the world of a Soviet fishing trawler (*Three Minutes of Silence,* 1969). He recreated each of these disparate realms with precision and candor, for the most part avoiding the cliches of construction novels and socialist realism.

The progression of Vladimov's works, as is the case with most good Soviet Russian writers, is fairly easy to see in retrospect. The career begins with a subject, at least, which is acceptable, even traditional; and each successive work strains the boundaries of the acceptable a little more. The characters become less conventional, the themes less predictable, the form less cliched. Behind the scenes the battles over what will be cut grow more intense. At some point the editors and superintendents cannot accept it any longer, and the writer is forced either to capitulate or to accept silence at home. In Vladimov's case, after years of editorial battles, he wrote a noble letter to the Union of Writers excoriating them, saying the only honorable path for a Soviet writer was to resign from the Union of Writers—and he returned his membership card. He was blacklisted everywhere, and *Faithful Ruslan* was published by Possev in Germany in 1975. A few weeks ago Vladimov was summoned to Lefortovo Prison in Moscow and interrogated for several hours. Later that day he had a heart attack. He was still in the hospital as of this original writing in 1980. However, by 1983 he was released; his new task as editor of the emigre journal *Facets* has already had salubrious results.

II.

There is another kind of Soviet writer who does not have to worry about hospital beds or prison cots. Semiliterate though many of them are, unread as they are, their works are printed in editions of hundreds of thousands of copies—by official decisions overseen by the Party officers and KGB (who are attached to every publishing house and the Union of Writers). It doesn't matter how many of the 100,000 copies are bought; the main thing is that the ideology be right, so the writer is paid a royalty for 100,000 and the editor of the publishing house is paid for fulfilling his plan. These are the kinds of writers—and often they are also secretaries of the local writers' unions—who are often sent to American-Soviet literary conferences. The most recent of four meetings was in Los Angeles in November. The American and the Soviet sponsors say these round-table meetings are intended to deepen mutual understanding. Is there, in fact, frank dialogue between equals? We send writers such as Joyce Carol Oates, John Updike, and Kurt Vonnegut; the Soviets send Party functionaries and hopeless Stalinist hacks. The American writers, who are not prepared in advance for what they will face, are puzzled and embarrassed because they don't know the names of their counterparts—and the Soviets say, "See, Americans don't know Soviet literature at all." After the first United States meeting, one American writer whom I had occasionally helped before with information about Russian affairs wrote me, concerned about why these nice, earnest fellow writers were not known here. What is happening, of course, is that the American writers are being misled and used. When their names appear beside those of the Party hacks in the official Soviet newspapers, the Soviet reader is supposed to think: well, everything's normal, our writers go there, theirs come here, they all talk as equals.

The official Soviet press report on the Los Angeles meeting shows clearly how the Soviets use such meetings. This bulletin appears on the front page of *Literary Gazette* for November 19 (in itself very unusual for these days, for Americans are virtually never mentioned on page one, even negatively), right beside two official resolutions of the Presidium, signed by Brezhnev, granting literary medals to two loyal drudges—one getting the "Order of the October Revolution," the other just the "Order of Friendship among Peoples." The report, in full, reads as follows:

122

The Soviet and American Writers' "Round Table"

The fourth meeting between Soviet and American writers which just took place in Los Angeles was a notable event in Soviet-American cultural cooperation. Headed by the editor-in-chief of *Foreign Literature,* N. Fedorenko, the Soviet delegation included G. Abashidze, D. Granin, V. Korotich, A. Ivanov, M. Slutskis, I. Stadnyuk, I. Zorina, and Ya. Zasursky. Participants from the American side of the meeting were the editor of the magazine *Saturday Review,* N. Cousins, and also R. Bradbury, E. Albee, E. Doctorow, E. Hardwick, H. Salisbury and others.

"Universal spiritual values and literature—such was the theme of our meeting," said N. Fedorenko in his interview with the TASS correspondent in San Francisco. "But it also touched on questions which go beyond the boundaries of this theme and concerned current problems of contemporaneity in the context of the present-day international situation. The Soviet and the American writers underlined the essential need for a dialogue between the peoples of our countries, the urgency of new efforts to forestall the arms race and to preserve peace as the main condition for the creation and production of spiritual values."

The participants of the round table criticized the new nuclear strategy of the American administration, a strategy allowing the possibility of "limited" nuclear war. The writers pointed out that in practice this kind of politics could lead to general thermonuclear catastrophe, to the destruction of universal human values created over the course of many centuries.

While understanding many current problems differently, the participants of the round table found points of contact and a common language on the question of the essential need to lessen international tension and return to a dialogue in accord with the spirit of the Helsinki Accords. In many speeches the lofty responsibility of the writer in the contemporary world was mentioned, as was the essential need for the writers to use all means available to them to continue the struggle for the preservation of peace on earth, the strengthening of cooperation.

The participants in the round table concurred that the meetings between American and Soviet writers should be continued with the goal of deepening mutual understanding.

The average Soviet reader will take this, among other things, as confirmation of his country's version of current politics, i.e., the Americans want to stir up a war psychosis, the CIA started invading Afghanistan, but Soviet policy is for peace, and this shows that Russians are trying to achieve peace—and that even well-known American writers agree with our point of view.

The American organizers of these meetings have sometimes urged American writers to mollify their counterparts, not to confront the Soviets openly and publicly. For example, when our delegation went to the USSR in 1979, the scandal over the *Metropole* anthology was in progress. The Americans were urged not to bring this up formally.

In Los Angeles, Edward Albee was the only one to address the Soviets as frankly as one would normally address equals (as opposed to coddled guests). He made a strong attack on them, asking about official retaliation against dissidents. The reply at first was stunned silence. Then Fedorenko (former Soviet ambassador to China and the U.N., to show what kind of writer he is) tried to pass it off by acting as if Albee were a naughty little boy. Fedorenko's formulaic assertion that the so-called dissidents are not really writers, but common criminals, goes back to the 1978 Soviet-American round table. Since they are criminals, they are of no concern to American writers. And so the conference moved majestically on to its topic: "Spiritual Values in Literature."

I should note that even by Soviet standards this latest Soviet delegation was something of a joke. Only Granin, or conceivably Slutskis, might reasonably be considered a writer of any standing. Ivanov and the rest are Union of Writers bully-boys—secretaries of the various branches of the union, editors (censors) of journals, trusted tools. Imagine that we were to send some mid-level Teamster officials and their enforcers to the USSR to discuss spiritual values in literature, and you will have a rough idea of what the Russians sent us. Of course, the Russians know this is all a farce, and they laugh at anyone who takes it seriously. They cover themselves by including one Americanist each time—Zasursky is a specialist on Western literature, a knowledgeable lackey who toes the Party line on every question even before it is laid down. His job is to speak English, show he reads things, and charm the natives.

Such trips to the United States are the most highly sought prizes among Soviet literary superintendents. The make-up of all such delegations is controlled by one man in the Central Committee of the Communist Party—Albert Belyaev, the true boss of all Soviet literature. Born in the town of Dirt (to translate the name), this all-powerful bureaucrat and former criminal (according to Kuznetsov's stories to intimates) became a specialist in "ideological warfare" in American proletarian novels of the 1930s, and now passes or rejects writers' applications for foreign passports. Since so few have opportunities for any trip abroad, never mind one that puts them at the same table with writers famous all over the world, they are always on their best behavior. And from the point of view of the bosses, these conferences serve two important purposes: (1) reward of the loyal old dogs, (2) something to report in the papers—i.e., a conference took place (showing not only "we are normal," but that the Helsinki Accords are being carried out faithfully).

So the answer to the question in the title of the essay is, yes, there are writers in the Soviet Union, and some of them are very talented. There are many others who are very good at writing what they are told to write. But the brain drain of the last eight years is almost without parallel. Among the most translated and visible writers who have left the USSR are Aksyonov, Aleshkovsky, Brodsky, Dovlatov, Galich, Gladilin, Gorbanevskaya, Maximov, Nekrasov, Sinyavsky, Sokolov, Solzhenitsyn, Suslov, Vladimov, Voinovich and Zinoviev. Fewer and fewer independent minds remain in the USSR; they work under ever more stringent restraints. And they are surrounded by the mass of Party careerists who are mainly interested in the many material rewards that the Union of Writers controls. To get trips, vacations, housing, cars, medical care, and tables at private restaurants, all doled out by the union's secretaries, the obedient writers are anxious to serve as good servants should serve—on their knees.

1981

The Remarkable Decade That Destroyed Russian Emigre Literature

Although it shows the timidity and ignorance of thirty-odd American publishers, it is of no real importance for the history of American literature that *Lolita* was first published in Paris. Victor Hugo spent twenty years in exile on the islands of Jersey and Guernsey; he wrote and published *Les Misérables* then, but no one calls it emigre literature. In 1855 a Russian exile wrote from England:

> A year ago I published part of my memoirs in Russian in London . . . I did not reckon upon readers nor upon any attention outside Russia. The success of the book exceeded all expectations . . . Let the secret and open police, who have been so well protected from publicity by the censorship and paternal punishments, know that sooner or later their deeds will come into the light of day.

I doubt that it would occur to anyone to exclude Herzen's *My Past and Thoughts* from a history of Russian letters, or to isolate it by terming it "emigre writing."

Indeed, the very term "emigre literature" is demeaning. It smacks of the ghetto. It suggests something limited, narrow, parochial, perhaps of interest for a time, but with no hope of entering the permanent culture of a language. If writers are *only* "emigre writers," they will probably be forgotten. "Emigre" literature is by definition a minority literature, a literature of special pleading, and like other defensive, minority types of literature—women's literature, gay literature, the literature of Michigan's Northern Peninsula—the attributive adjective itself determines its final fate—the compost heap of culture. Emigre literature is detritus. Emigre poetry is Yury Mandelstam, not Osip Mandelstam. Emigre literature is *yat'* and *tverdyi znak*. Emigre literature is critical rejection of Nabokov's novels. Emigre literature is graphomaniacs like Merezhkovsky and Gippius shining Mussolini's boots. Emigre literature is *Novoe russkoe slovo* refusing to print a mild excerpt from Aksyonov's *The Burn* because of its language.

The Burn, however, is not emigre literature, in spite of the place of publication or the location of the author's body at the instant of publication. Aksyonov is one of the many important writers who have done the service of destroying what was left of emigre literature and beginning a unique new era in Russian literature. They have created not emigre literature, and not Soviet literature, but simply Russian literature. In this sense, though we need not be slaves to round numbers, the decade of the seventies was a remarkable one, with such landmarks as Nadezhda Mandelstam's memoirs and *Metropole* standing at either end.

In the sixties emigre literature was approaching senility. The prolific old Chekhov Publishing House had long since been closed. Biology took its toll on the first generation, and the second wave had no writers of international stature. The Iron Curtain was still the Iron Curtain. True, there were some intimations of transition: the minor sensations of Tarsis and Kuznetsov, the appearance of an ambiguous fellow named Abram Tertz, and the first book by Joseph Brodsky. But even in May 1972 when Brodsky sat with his friends from Ann Arbor on a remote section of the roof of the Peter-Paul Fortress, and was assured that he could become poet-in-residence at the University of Michigan, no one could have predicted what would happen in the remainder of the decade.

A vast new flow of people and books began. Writers sent manuscripts abroad for publication; some lied about it—and got away with it. Others didn't bother to lie, and even they got away with it; they published abroad not only once, but repeatedly, and still held onto their Moscow apartments—if not always their telephones. Drawers and archives emptied out, their contents were printed and shipped right back to the Soviet Union. A large part, in many ways the best part, of Soviet Russian literature simply moved abroad for one stage of its existence—the printing stage. What one had as a result of this was not emigre literature, but a book distribution problem, a marketing dilemma. Writers born in the USSR, speaking Soviet Russian, writing primarily of Soviet life, and writing for the audience which shared that life, now dominate Russian literature. Their achievements are the ones which will remain in their culture.

The remarkable decade of the 1970s brought us the best Russian writing in almost fifty years. The litany of titles is a long one—in poetry, fiction, and historical writing. Exile literature tends to be a characteristic of underdeveloped nations, third-world countries. They know more about it in Asia, Africa, and South America than we do. Nevertheless, Russians find themselves, like all these other numerous emigres, specializing in the two most popular and common modes of writing in exile: simple testimony and violent denunciation. Thus we have a vast new literature of memoirs and documents: *The Gulag Archipelago*, Nadezhda Mandelstam, Evgenia Ginzburg, Kopelev, Amalrik, Litvinov, Chalidze, Bukovsky, the marvelous periodicals *Memory* and *Searchings*, some of whose editors are still in the USSR.

Individual achievements in poetry and prose fiction are also impressive. There are old names and new names, traditional styles and experimental works, Socialist Realism straight up and Socialist Realism inside out. Some of the authors live abroad, some do not. Some publish partly abroad, some only abroad. They represent different generations. I cannot imagine writing a history of Russian literature in the seventies and not including such writers such as Aksyonov, Bitov, Brodsky, Iskander, Sinyavsky, Sokolov, Solzhenitsyn, Vladimov, or Voinovich. Then again, I cannot imagine writing a history of twentieth-century Russian literature and not devoting generous space to Bunin, Tsvetaeva, Khodasevich, and Nabokov. *But the fact is that not a single standard history of twentieth-century Russian literature does this.*

The last two generations of histories of literature have regularly excluded writers who lived or published abroad for long periods, and this is a mistake I hope will not be made in the next histories. Remember that twenty years ago what was called emigre literature was scarcely studied at all. In the 1960s at the University of Michigan, my teachers did not mention the existence of any emigre writers. Gradually I got the vaguest notions of Russian writers abroad— Pninian visions of sad incompetents watching their clothes go round in the dryer. The odd issue of *Novyi zhurnal* or the Russian newspapers, getting more boring and repetitive all the time, with funeral announcements boxing out the living world, did not enliven these impressions.

This is not just a thing of the past. In the supposedly authoritative *Introduction to Russian Language and Literature* published by the Cambridge University Press in 1977, there is no substantive treatment of Tsvetaeva, Nabokov, or Khodasevich—although Kazin and Gerasimov, along with dozens of other drudges, are noted, just because of the location of their publishing houses and their having belonged to a group. In this area Western scholars blindly followed Soviet official practice.

I believe that the would-be historian of Russian letters should understand that if one uses anything but language as a criterion for whom to include, the contradictions become hopelessly irreconcilable.

If you would call Aksyonov an emigre writer, how would you decide which of his works are emigre ones. He was born a Soviet citizen of good Soviet parents. He was nurtured on good Soviet life—from Magadan to the Palace of Congresses—nay, even *beyond* the Palace of Congresses—the Ts.D. L. (Central House of Literators). He not only spoke their language, he *revealed* it to his generation. So was he an emigre when he wrote "The Steel Bird," when it came out in *Glagol* in 1977, or was it when *The Burn* was written, or when he played the role of glue in the group effort which led to the first edition of *Metropole?* Or when that same anthology was photographically reprinted (does photography change the essence of literature)? Or when it was newly typeset perhaps? Maybe when Aksyonov's citizenship was revoked? No, to use a Soviet sequence of tenses—he was a Soviet Russian writer, he is a Soviet Russian writer, and he always will be a Soviet Russian writer.

One can ask the same questions of virtually all of the writers present. Was Sasha Sokolov an emigre when he sat on the banks of the Volga in the mid-1970s, writing *A School for Fools* with no hope of ever publishing such a dreamy book? What could be less emigre than his hymn to the Russian language *Between the Dog and the Wolf?*

Is Voinovich an emigre Russian writer? When did he become one, if so? Perhaps years ago in Poland when he saw the real-life drunken Chonkin being dragged along under a cart? Or when he got off the plane in Munich? Such questions make the term "emigre" writer, as it is normally used, seem meaningless. Did Pasternak become an emigre when *Doctor Zhivago* was published abroad? Is Vladimov more or less an emigre writer than Zinoviev, Erofeev, or Aleshkovsky? Whom does Aksyonov have more in common with—Bitov and Iskander, or Muravin and Dubrovin? And even Solzhenitsyn has much more in common with Sholokhov than with Leonid Rzhevsky.

No, there is only one Russian literature that matters—and this is it, folks. It's all around the hemisphere, without any borders outside of grammar. In spite of the forests felled to keep the Markovs and Bondarevs going, they'll be lucky to get asterisks in the history of

Russian literature. But the genuine writers—wherever their weary bones and brains are located at the moment they conceive, or write, or photocopy, or publish their works—will survive, and the best of these will even flourish.

Some writers are worried about their seemingly diminished audience. Some may even have to publish themselves. Well, publishing oneself is not all a bad tradition. Dostoevsky published himself; so did Walt Whitman, Proust, and Virginia Woolf. And in the end it doesn't matter at all; the world still reads *The Devils, Leaves of Grass,* and *Remembrance of Things Past.*

The size of the edition doesn't matter much either. Many writers feel they are writing in a vacuum if only 1000 or 5000 copies of a book are printed. They are simply spoiled by Soviet print-runs. There is very little correlation between numbers of books printed and a book's longevity or influence. Hundreds of books are printed in editions of 100,000 in this country every year, and they are forgotten by the end of the year.

On the other hand only 1200 copies of Delvig's *Northern Flowers* were printed, and it has not been forgotten. The first edition of *Dead Souls* in 1842 was only 2400 copies, *The Devils* only 3400. The first edition of *Ulysses* was a mere 1000. *Moby Dick*'s first edition sold a quick 2000 copies but it was generally misunderstood and disliked, and sales fell so rapidly that when a fire destroyed the stock two years later Harper's refused to reprint it.

Print-runs are of tertiary importance. Good writing is a powerful dye; once it gets into the solution, it penetrates everything—and it's hard to expunge. To use an economic metaphor, good books drive out bad.

Moreover, Russian books published outside the USSR are far from meaningless even quantitatively. I estimate that at least 200 books and journals are produced annually. Assuming print-runs of from 1000 to 5000 and, say, an average of 2000 copies, that is over 200,000 books every year. An educated guess is that between 20 and 30 percent of these books ultimately go into the Soviet Union. Thus roughly 50,000 copies cross the border yearly. Assume that each is read by ten people—and some by as many as a hundred people—and you see the potential readership is substantial.

If one is determined to influence literary conventions, it is even more important to know who these readers are. The factory worker in Vladivostok is obviously less likely to read *Continent* than is a member of the Union of Writers in Moscow. It is clear that the literary world that read Solzhenitsyn and Nekrasov in the past will continue to read them in the future. Books published abroad have a strong influence on good writers still living in the Soviet Union. For example, I cannot imagine Bitov's *Pushkin House* without Nabokov's *The Gift*. And every young poet in Leningrad has Brodsky staring him in the face.

Tamizdat influences Gosizdat in other ways, too. The widespread printing and translation of works by now safely dead classics, such as Akhmatova, Mandelstam, Bulgakov, Pasternak, and Tsvetaeva, no doubt no doubt prompted earlier and more extensive publication of the same authors in the Soviet Union. Once the Possev edition of *The Master and Margarita* was being smuggled in and was well known, nothing serious stood in the way of a full edition at home. Better to give a sanitized version of *A Poem without a Hero* than to allow the real one to stand alone.

Convergence in the literary sphere is already a very strong phenomenon, but when my posited unified history of Russian letters will finally be written I cannot say. Perhaps in twenty, or fifty, or a hundred years—but it will happen, because the Soviet system will change. All things do, and it certainly will, because it is inherently mendacious, mediocre, and weak.

Seeing Soviet Marxism as an almost cosmic incarnation of evil merely contributes to its continuing power. A less apocalyptic view is that the USSR is just the world's biggest banana republic. The way nations get free of dictators who award themselves literary prizes (among others) is well known. Neo-Dostoevskian mumbo-jumbo about the forces of darkness, and the dangers of too much freedom for individuals, and so on is self-defeating.

When Russians, like the Poles, fully realize this, the new revolution can occur almost overnight. And then the literary rubbish will be swept away rapidly. The culture now being created outside the control of a Party oligarchy will assume its natural place. The literature that is left will have only one basic adjective to describe it: Russian.

[A speech delivered at the conference "Russian Literature in Emigration: The Third Wave," *1981*]

A Footnote to the Zhivago Affair
or
Ann Arbor's Strange Connections with Russian Literature

Superstition, if it were more a part of my make-up, would force me to believe that there were some ultramundane magnets at work drawing Russian literature to Ann Arbor. Geography, ethnography, and population all made it unlikely that Ardis, the largest publisher of Russian books outside the USSR, should be born and flourish in this "provincial" (as the Russians would call it) town. In the 1970s and 1980s many celebrated Russian writers either lived in Ann Arbor or interrupted complex continental itineraries to make the trip to Ardis and speak at the University of Michigan. True, the famous White General Denikin is buried here, and the odd noun "Michigander" has something Gogolian about it, but such parallels are too flimsy to create the magnetic field I hypothesize.

Whatever the cause, Ann Arbor was linked with Russian writers even before Ardis was founded in 1971. Perhaps the beginning of the connection was an event that occurred just after I arrived in Ann Arbor as a freshman and first heard a lecture given by the brilliant Byzantinist, Ihor Shevchenko. The lecture, suitably enough, was on the Futurists and Pasternak.

The *Zhivago* affair must be seen in the context of Soviet attitudes toward publication abroad. From the start—October 1917—it was dangerous business for a Soviet writer to publish abroad. Also from the start, the Bolshevik regime's uncertainty of purpose, copyright complications, and the avatar's desire to seem liberal led to some sanctioned printing of Soviet writers abroad. Sometimes the foreign publications were ignored, sometimes they were used against the writers. In the early 1920s the two books of poetry which established Pasternak's reputation were both printed outside of Russia.

My Sister, Life, Pasternak's most famous book, was published in

1921 by Grzhebin Publishers, with the place of publication given as "Berlin-Petersburg-Moscow," despite the fact that the books were all manufactured in Berlin. This was the confused early period of Soviet control over literature, but things rapidly became clear. Pasternak was in Berlin when Helikon published his *Themes and Variations*, an edition which listed place of publication as "Moscow-Berlin." Before Pasternak left Berlin for Moscow he took all of his copies and carefully inked out the offensive word "Berlin." (The Ardis facsimile edition was made from one of these doctored copies.) Pasternak was aware as early as this that the times had changed, that the ambiguous practice of foreign publication was becoming too dangerous. By the end of the 1920s Russian writers had been taught that publication abroad would lead to exile and worse, that it was not congruent with censorship, and that the true Iron Age had begun.

Then something extraordinary happened. Under complicated circumstances, including a promise from someone in authority that the work would be published in the USSR in some form, Pasternak released a copy of the manucript of *Doctor Zhivago* for foreign publication—but only in translation. In his 1956 contract with the Italian Communist publisher Feltrinelli, he specifically did *not* give Russian rights to anyone outside of the USSR. Nevertheless, in 1958 the University of Michigan Press published the Russian text, which stayed in print through many editions, and in 1960 was actually corrected by Pasternak's trusted friend Countess de Proyart, and corrected using an authorized manuscript.

An interesting background for what is to follow is the behavior of Pasternak's family abroad. Most of his family, including his mother and famous painter father, had left Russia after the Revolution, but they had maintained fairly good relations with the regime, and had little trouble travelling back and forth, which indicates a special case. I believe there was a clear *quid pro quo* here. It is quite possible that the family resisted any attempts to publish a large body of unpublished materials, such as letters. Their policy seems to have been to wait for the large Soviet editions and keep really political material out of what was published in the West. Only in 1981 did readers have access to the Pasternak-Freidenberg letters, published in English as a Helen and Kurt Wolff book at Harcourt, Brace. That the family trusted the Wolffs will become clear below, but that Pasternak himself was pursuing a different policy from that of his emigre relatives (who were consistently more cautious, it would appear), will also become clear.

The University of Michigan Press also published what remains the finest and most nearly comprehensive edition of Pasternak's poetry and prose, edited by Gleb Struve and Boris Filippov. This entire project was without precedent for a university press. Struve and Filippov also compiled the standard editions of Mandelstam and Akhmatova, but these editions were published by the more or less fictitious "Inter-Language Literary Associates" which was largely, if not totally, funded by CIA fronts. Projects of such magnitude could not possibly be financially self-supporting, and would not be practical until changing technology transformed small-run publishing. Meantime, it was a remarkable aspect of an organization which has suffered so many self-inflicted wounds that the CIA should devote dollars to the classics of Soviet literature, few of which are political in our sense. No one who subsidizes books by Mandelstam and Akhmatova can be all bad.

As we were to learn much later, in 1980, the CIA connection was not far from the Michigan edition of *Doctor Zhivago* either. The fact is that the CIA and perhaps even the British intelligence services did play a direct (though erratic) role in the publication of the first Russian-language edition of the novel in 1958. It is fascinating to see how all of this developed, but this story is of little importance compared to the importance of the text itself. Russian literature is rich in examples of important works published abroad under peculiar circumstances. The Tsar's censors and bishops, for example, prevented many of Tolstoi's most important works from being printed legally in Russian for over thirty years. Such works as *What is Art?* could be published in full only in free countries such as England or Germany. This, too, is an interesting story *historically;* this, too, involves the secret police, manuscript smuggling to the West, and the smuggling of the finished books back to the East. But the *texts* for which people made sacrifices are what matters. Even today, it would be virtually impossible to find any of Tolstoi's banned works of 1881-1910 printed as separate books in the Soviet Union since the Revolution. They are safely tucked away in the ninety-volume Jubilee Edition, available only at the best libraries (and one cannot take books out of Soviet libraries). If one has the idea that one might obtain *The Kingdom of God Is Within You* or *What's To Be Done?* at even the central monasteries, one had better think again.

Laurence Sterne not completely aside, the prologue to the story of the publication of *Doctor Zhivago* is no less fantastic in its connections to significant events in Russian literature than the actual story of the novel itself. The thread extends back to France and Switzerland of the 1930s and the assassination of a former Comintern secret agent. The man known as "Ignace Reiss" was murdered, his bullet-ridden body found on the outskirts of Lausanne in September 1937. One of the people who took part in the surveillance and organization of this murder (as well as that of Trotsky's son, Andrei Sedov) was Sergei Efron, husband of Marina Tsvetaeva, one of Russia's greatest poets— and a friend of Pasternak's. Efron disappeared into Spain, then returned to Moscow, where he himself was executed. Tsvetaeva, against the advice of many people, returned to Russia herself in 1939, unaware of what she should expect, partly because Pasternak, when he saw her in Paris in 1935, failed to give her a good idea of what she should expect. He later blamed himself for this, but never really explained. How do we get from Ignace Reiss, Efron, Tsvetaeva, and Pasternak in the 1930s to Ann Arbor?

Reiss's real name was Poretsky, and his widow was Elsa Bernaut, who published the memoirs *Our Own People* under the name Elizabeth Poretsky, a book first published in English by the University of Michigan Press. The murder of her husband was one of the final steps in Elsa Bernaut's natural conversion to new beliefs and a desire to work against the Soviet government which devoured its own. Some time in the 1950s, according to the American publisher Felix Morrow, Bernaut became a consultant to the CIA. One of the things she was interested in was getting free books to Soviet readers to show them some of the variety and independence of thought which exists in the world.

It is a secret, but not a very secret secret, that the CIA has subsidized wholly or partially a number of publications, journals and books, at least since the 1950s. The revelation that *Encounter* was partly supported by them was one of the post-Vietnam scandals among liberals at a time when many activities, both good and bad, became public. (A few consistent hobgoblins saw even the CIA's good deeds as bad.) In my field it is well-known that various publications in English and Russian have been supported in this way, most of them taking the form of books to be smuggled into the Soviet Union. The vast majority of these books were not political in the Western sense. In the case of publishers such as Ardis (and there are a number now), who accept no such support, there exist organization book handlers who order, pay for and then distribute every sort of book not published in the USSR: Mandelstam, Pasternak, Akhmatova, Zamyatin, Solzhenitsyn, translations of Orwell, translations of Western studies of Russian historical figures—the list is endless and sad. Books smuggled by Soviet seamen and diplomats, friendly Italian Communist tourists,

135

reporters and students of all nations include modern works by Aksyonov, Brodsky, Voinovich and the entire "Third Wave" of emigres, as well as translations of current, but unacceptable bestsellers such as *Gorky Park*.

When the CIA started this work, apparently in the 1950s, they had no experience, and needed assistance in the world of publishing. Reiss's widow Elsa Bernaut turned to Felix Morrow for help. Morrow was once a leading American Trotskyite, and after 1946 simply a democratic socialist working in the field of publishing. As Mr. Morrow explained when he first wrote to me on October 6, 1980, Elsa and he had had occasion to meet a number of the leading CIA people. He made two conditions: he would never receive any compensation, and they would never ask him anything about the Trotskyite movement.

Now we come to late 1957 or early 1958, when Elsa asked Morrow to meet with the CIA Deputy Chief of Security, who asked him to take on what Morrow called an "astonishing and attractive task." They wanted him to take the manuscript of *Doctor Zhivago*, which they had acquired, and have it typeset in the United States in a Russian typeface not used here. Then he was to take the proofs to Europe and have an edition of the novel printed there. I speculate that aside from the fact that the books would be distributed in Europe, the other main reason to have them printed there was to avoid an edition using American paper, which would immediately have given away the country of origin.

This was all to be done in time to distribute copies at the World's Fair in Brussels during the summer and fall of 1958. There was a Soviet Pavilion, and many Soviet visitors were expected. Morrow remembers dealing with Catholics, so I conclude that it is precisely the edition which he arranged that was distributed with such manic success at the Vatican Pavilion by Russian-speaking priests. Max Hayward, who did not know about the CIA edition, describes (in his notes to Ivinskaya's *A Captive of Time*) the mysterious appearance of this blue-bound novel at the Fair, Feltrinelli's puzzlement, and the way copies quickly made their way to Russia. (I also attended this fair in September 1958, and while I did not feel drawn to the Vatican exhibit, I did purchase a different kind of literary contraband, banned in the *West*: the Olympia edition of *Lolita*, then subject to confiscation in many countries, and later to be pushed off American bestseller lists by—*Doctor Zhivago*.)

But I am jumping ahead of the full story. Let us back up. Morrow agreed to the CIA's proposal and had *Doctor Zhivago* typeset by Rausen, a Menshevik Russian typesetting company in New York. The next step was to arrange the printing itself. He contacted a former associate of Sneevliet in Holland, and this person provided what was supposed to be a safe Dutch printing plant. Guy de Mallac and Ronald Hingley in their books on Pasternak mention that another unauthorized Russian edition of the novel was printed in Holland by Mouton & Co., possibly from the same proofs Morrow had provided, but it seems more likely that there was no such printing, but rather that a title page may have been added to deflect suspicion. I have yet to see any copies of this. However, at the very moment when Morrow had the Holland printing ready to go, the CIA inexplicably began to put the brakes on the whole project, partly by withholding printing money.

A number of questions arise. First of all, where did the CIA get its manuscript of the novel, the one given to Morrow in typescript form? Is there any way to determine how many copies of the Russian typescript there were in the West? The first question has a fascinating answer: the manuscript passed to Morrow, he was told, came via British Intelligence. The latter had supposedly arranged for a plane carrying Feltrinelli and the manucript to be diverted to Malta for an emergency stop. There his baggage was searched and the manuscript was photographed. Morrow recalls that it was a Moscow-Italy flight. However, other sources agree that Sergio d'Angelo was the person to whom Pasternak gave the manuscript in May 1956, and that d'Angelo gave it to Feltrinelli in Berlin. It would therefore have to be a Berlin-Italy flight, one which hardly would be diverted to Malta. On the other hand, it may be that the entire d'Angelo story which has come to be accepted is nothing but a total fabrication which succeeded in becoming part of the *Doctor Zhivago* lore. Perhaps Feltrinelli got the first manuscript in an entirely different way.

But we still have the second question of how many copies were floating around. This is difficult to answer. One widely-accepted story is that by mid-1956 word of the novel was quite widespread. Pasternak gave his manuscript to Italian Communist d'Angelo (a scout for Feltrinelli who had been working for Radio Moscow) in May 1956 with serious forebodings, although it was the month that Fadeev committed suicide, and only a few months after Khrushchev's "Secret Speech"; in other words, during the "Thaw." It is also accepted that not many days later the manuscript was passed to Feltrinelli in Berlin, and that Pasternak signed a contract with Feltrinelli June 13, 1956, granting him everything but Russian-language rights. Until January of 1957 Pasternak apparently believed that some kind of Russian edition, perhaps censored, would be done in the Soviet Union. Until the Hungarian Revolution, it was a fairly liberal year, and his works were being sought for print. By February 1957 this dream was over.

Another copy reached the West through Countess Jacqueline de Proyart, a Harvard Ph.D. and head of the Tolstoi Museum in Paris. She met Pasternak January 1, 1957, and a friendship quickly developed. The writer gave her power-of-attorney to look after his rights in the West on February 7, an act which caused some divisiveness. De Proyart was given a manuscript of the novel which had previously been in the hands of the very official writer Simonov—afterwards referred to as "the Simonov manuscript." De Proyart smuggled the manuscript out and took this copy to Gallimard Publishers. Another manuscript had also been in the keeping of the Soviet State Publishers, Goslitizdat, since 1955. Given the normal practices of samizdat in Russia, it is quite possible that the manuscript had multiplied from the start. Even discounting the Malta version, it is very possible that the manuscript had been copied in Italy—indeed, it is hard to imagine that this did *not* happen. The same could happen at Gallimard, and as time went by and translation rights were sold, many copies had to be made.

There is general agreement that the first edition published was the Italian translation, which came out in November 1957. Hingley mentions that the Russian text was published in Italy shortly thereafter, and de Mallac writes that Feltrinelli published a Russian edition in 1957. I think both of these sources are wrong, and that Feltrinelli indeed kept his promise not to publish the book in Russian. The evidence for this follows below.

But let us return to the CIA. Whatever the provenance of their manuscript, why did the CIA refuse Morrow permission to go ahead with the next stages of the book at this point, before the Brussels Fair? Morrow recalls a peculiar string of weak excuses. They claimed they couldn't get clearance from the Russian Desk, then they wanted a check on the proofs for possible errors (although he had already had this done), then they began an investigation to make certain that the Russian typeface used "was not of U. S. origin." Morrow had already made sure of this as well. Finally the go-ahead was given for the manufacture of the first edition, and the books were delivered to Brussels on the next to last day before the Fair. The Vatican connection, presumably, was complete.

Then there was another sudden change. Morrow remembers: "I had also been asked to make arrangements with anti-Stalinist trade unionists in Amsterdam and Brussels to distribute copies of the book at nominal cost to sailors on Russian-bound ships but this was taken out of my hands just after the books were manufactured."

Morrow began to think that the CIA had lost interest in the project, and later decided that not many of them were smart enough to see the long-term literary importance of the book. He saw no reason why a reputable United States publisher, preferably a university press, should not publish an edition of the Russian *Doctor Zhivago* for a wide audience. He formally proposed to the CIA that he be given permission to arrange for such publication at the University of Michigan Press, which was headed by his friend Fred Wieck. Months passed without an answer. Meantime Feltrinelli made it clear that he would never issue a Russian-language edition because it would anger the Soviets, and at one time Pasternak had been against it. He was, however, supposedly going to produce a small edition in Russian "so that the twelve or fourteen reviewers who are expert in Russian can appraise the literary quality of the work," according to a *New York Times* story of November 2, 1958.

Morrow understood that Feltrinelli would never do the edition, even if Pasternak asked him to. Morrow decided to go ahead, but the CIA objected: "In the end I could get no permission and I decided to act on my own. Fred Wieck and I got the express permission of President Hatcher of the University of Michigan. The royalties were to be held for disposal by Pasternak. The CIA sent one emissary after another to Wieck and Hatcher, who stood their ground and refused to agree to the urging of the CIA that we not publish the book. It was published and now, 21 years later, is still in print at Michigan" (letter of October 6, 1980).

I asked Mr. Morrow to clarify a number of points, and in September of 1982 he wrote me that he had tried to examine the files at both the University of Michigan and Harcourt, Brace, Jovanovich. Michigan was cooperative. William Jovanovich, however, wrote Morrow December 12, 1980, rejecting his request to review the *Doctor Zhivago* files on the grounds that Helen Wolff was strongly against it. At this point Morrow explained that among those who had objected to the Michigan edition of the novel were Feltrinelli and the Wolffs. Feltrinelli refused Michigan a license. When the Italian version appeared Feltrinelli announced that the only way the Russian could be published was if the Soviet Union of Writers allowed it. Of course Feltrinelli walked a fine line between the demands of the Italian Communist Party (Togliatti tried to dissuade him from any publication) and his own sense that the novel must be published.

Pasternak had already understood that his hopes for a Soviet edition were to be disappointed, and that very same Union of Writers had begun the attacks which ended in his exclusion from that organization. So at this point, the behavior of Feltrinelli and the Wolffs is a little confusing. Kurt Wolff wrote to the University of Michigan Press on November 12, 1958, trying to get them to halt preparations for the Russian text. As Morrow writes:

> Helen and Kurt Wolff claimed that Michigan's publication of the Russian language *Zhivago* would jeopardize all Pasternak's copyrights. This was a different argument from Feltrinelli's claim of the jurisdiction of the Soviet Writers' Union, but neither I nor anyone else has ever been able to make any sense out of the Wolff objections. It was clear to Fred Wieck and me that one could copyright translations of *Zhivago* but that the Russian language version could not be copyrighted in the USA because U. S. copyright law permits no copyright of Russian work by a Russian national because there is no copyright agreement between the two countries. [The Soviet Union joined the Copyright Convention in 1973, CRP.] When we finally forced Feltrinelli to grant us a license, in turn we agreed to apply for a U. S. copyright for the Russian language version, but we knew it was a futile gesture.

Wieck wrote to the copyright office on December 4, 1959, saying "Our Italian colleague strongly resisted Russian publication on this side of the Iron Curtain and yielded only to our earnest and persistent demand that this work had to be made available in the original version. If our Italian colleague had not yielded, Michigan would have published anyway."

Pasternak made his decision when he handed over the Russian manuscript—that was the crucial moment. As many eyewitness accounts agree, he had the sense that he had done something fateful, and there is no doubt that despite vacillation, the forced signing of protest telegrams and so on, he wished the novel to be published in as many languages as possible, including Russian, once the possibility of Soviet publication had evaporated. Feltrinelli is extremely unstable during this affair: he knew enough to ignore Pasternak's forced protest telegram, and resisted Togliatti's attempts to dissuade him from the original Italian publication, but balked at Michigan's doing the Russian, although he finally gave in. As for the other people in this story, they may have actually believed what the KGB always wants the West to believe, that Russian language publication will cause more trouble. But when a novel is front-page news around the world in translation, a few thousand copies in Russian are not decisive. Pasternak, as I say, had already taken the important step of sending the manuscript out. As someone who has often been in the position of receiving such works, I can say that it is almost unheard of that it would be done without the author being quite aware of the consequences of his action.

But this is not the end of the story. Michigan later prepared a corrected edition of the *Doctor Zhivago* text. Jacqueline de Proyart, Pasternak's agent, read the proofs for this corrected edition, and also provided the press with a microfilm of the proofs of the large volume of Pasternak's poetry which the Soviet publishing house Goslitizdat had prepared and then abandoned. This microfilm would then become the Press's edition of Pasternak's poetry, the production of which was planned in the summer of 1960. That all of this was provided indicates Pasternak's attitude to the University of Michigan's publication of *Doctor Zhivago*. This edition became the primary source, and still serves Russian readers all over the world—and it is mentioned in the *Soviet Literary Encyclopedia.*

When Struve wrote to Wieck about this edition and discussed the source of the materials that went into it, he said that both Pasternak and Countess de Proyart had serious doubts about Feltrinelli's honesty. He noted that Pasternak especially wished that any royalties from the Russian editon should remain in the United States and in no case be deposited in the bank which Feltrinelli used for Pasternak's account.

Doctor Zhivago, despite countless rumors that it will come out "soon," has not yet been published in the Soviet Union, but because of the Michigan edition virtually all members of the Soviet literary world have read it. All of the efforts to keep the Russian *Zhivago* out of print failed miserably.

The final scene in this drama is not without irony. In the 1980s Feltrinelli Editore (some ten years after Feltrinelli himself was the victim of a bomb) put on sale an undated and inexpensive paperback edition of the novel in Russian. The edition claims copyright and mentions the first Italian edition of 1957. Like every other so-called Feltrinelli edition, it is an exact photographic copy of the Michigan edition.

1984

Russian Writing and Border Guards: Twenty-five Years of the New Isolationism

Airline pilots are experts on Soviet attitudes toward borders, but we literary scholars also know a great deal about the subject. The isolationism typical of the post-Brezhnev era has had many little funny but tragic signposts. The "cultural newspapers" are full of these. For example, on December 9, 1981, *The Literary Gazette* reported in absolute seriousness on a Union of Writers Secretariat meeting devoted to "the theme of the relations between writers and border guards!" A competition for works in all genres on the MVD (Ministry of Internal Affairs) was also announced. Not very long ago one could take out of the Soviet Union any books printed after 1917 without special library permission; then the restriction rose to cover pre-1945 books—now customs agents are tougher coming and going: *no* books published before 1970 can be taken out without the laborious process of getting written permission from the Lenin Library. This is symbolic of the current Soviet attitude toward the movement of literature across its frontiers in either direction.

The same paranoia about books and foreigners pervades all other areas. Last year laws were introduced making Soviet citizens liable for trial if they tell "work" (*sluzhebnyi*) secrets to foreigners, i.e., a person who told a foreign friend a bread recipe or the shift schedule of a toy factory could be tried. Starting July 1, 1984, Russians who "help foreigners," for example, by giving then a ride in a private car or letting them spend the night at their apartment can be fined from 10 to 50 rubles. Such "services" and "secrets" are largely unspecified, so a Russian citizen does not really know what he can do or not—he just knows foreigners are trouble. They don't have to wear special uniforms as they did under Tsar Paul, but they are trouble.

For twenty-five or thirty years the shifts in official policies have been frequent and startling. Scarcely anyone would now dare say when exactly all the "thaws" were. What is publishable has varied spectacularly from journal to journal and year to year. One year Solzhenitsyn could get published and hope for a Lenin prize; another year he was thrown out of his country. In the early 1960s poets and singers such as Evtushenko, Voznesensky, Vysotsky and Okudzhava performed before crowds of thousands (even though Vysotsky was never allowed to publish or even to have a poster of announcement, and Okudzhava never was allowed a book of music); but now the two celebrated poets are obediently wealthy Soviet classics, while Vysotsky (who died in 1980) was first published in the illegal *Metropole* (1979) and Okudzhava, his only book of words and music published by Ardis, was careful, comfortable, and kind when he travelled abroad as an only slightly suspect representative of Soviet culture a few years ago.

The year 1977 was the height of cultural detente. The Soviets staged an international book fair at which Ardis was allowed to display Russian books by Nabokov, Brodsky and others for the first time in Soviet history; the Soviet copyright agency, VAAP, was actively buying rights to Western books; tens of thousands of Russians were being allowed to leave the country and telephone back to their friends unhindered. But by the end of 1979 everything had changed. Ardis was the only publishing house banned from the next Book Fair, where the number and kinds of Western books confiscated grew markedly; my wife and I and other American publishers were denied visas; VAAP assumed a defensive position and tried to stop Russians from publishing abroad; emigration ground to a virtual halt; and a large number of the Soviet phones were unplugged, and direct dialling stopped.

A neo-Stalinist, isolationist position is the one held today. One reason so-called "country prose" has many authoritative supporters is that it makes people look inwards and to the past rather than outwards and to the future; and even better, it can foster xenophobia. Influential literary power-brokers, such as Palievsky and Kozhinov, ideologues of the nationalistic Russite movement, influence what gets published; they help foster country prose—or foreign prose which they can interpret as showing the virtues of nationalism and the past. Isolationism is obvious on the political scene. The destruction of an international commercial airliner is the most obvious example, of course. But it is also clear from such things as: (1) the 1982 restrictions on international (and even inter-city!) telephones, introduced in two phases, reducing circuits by about three-quarters; (2) new restrictions on book exports introduced to cut the export of virtually all Soviet books, including those sold to foreigners in special dollar stores, restrictions which were introduced almost secretly in September 1982; (3) intensifying attacks on modern Western culture—everything from films such as *The Deer Hunter* (the Russians and their "friendly" bloc withdrew from the Berlin Film Festival in 1980 to protest its showing), *Gorky Park, Moscow on the Hudson* and most recently even Michael Jackson (pilloried in a June 1984 issue of the newspaper *Soviet Culture* for many sins, notably "forcing" people to look at his video and forget serious social problems); (4) a panoply of new customs rules (no longer can a man take in a skirt, no longer can one take a jar of caviar without a receipt from an official store) and searches of all kinds, for goods as well as "literature" have intensified; (5) the blithe ease with which Soviet theater authorities acting for the Central Committee took away their greatest theater director's theater (Yury Lubimov's Taganka) and gave it to a willing compromiser; (6) the best Soviet film director, Tarkovsky, asked for political asylum in July 1984. Because of the new climate of press vitriol and the successful creation of non-specific fear, rejected writers think far less often of the option of publishing abroad now.

The USSR is a nation which can always find a large supply of willing writers and quickly manufacture new classics to take the place of those who leave Russia (Brodsky, Solzhenitsyn, Voinovich, Aksyonov, Maximov—just to name a few who have been widely translated into English). Not only do they do this, but they also refuse to discuss it. And they ever so honestly declare in *The Literary Gazette* (July 15, 1981) that the two main centers of modern culture are Moscow and Paris! And this is proclaimed from a country in which *every* page of *every* proof must be signed and stamped in ink first by the editor and then by the censor before it can be printed—whether the page is instructions for a sausage grinder or the first page of another epic novel on the meaning of Soviet history from Yalta to the signing of the Helsinki accords. This description is not a joke. It is a toned-down version of the descriptions from *New Books,* the central advance book announcements of the USSR, which describe Books 1, 2, and 3 of Chakovsky's forthcoming (1984-85) blockbuster, *Victory.* So it's no surprise that copying machines are all in locked, windowless rooms. It's more of a surprise that even many emigre Russian writers insist that their modern literature is superior to American and other Western literatures now.

We can make a few fairly safe generalizations about the themes, characters, and style which dominated in these works written roughly between 1960 and the present. The two basic facts of writers' and all Russians' existence were (1) Stalin, and (2) War. The internal dictator decimated his enemies and his friends with the Great Terror; then an external dictator laid waste to much of the land and its population. Arguments are still going on about who killed more millions of people—Stalin or Hitler.

It is peculiar that one of these basic facts—World War II (which in the USSR is always called the "Great Patriotic War")—is the subject of a great mass of official Soviet literature, as represented by Bondarev, Abramov, Zalygin, and countless others. (War is a common theme in emigre prose as well.) The other basic fact, the archipelago of camps, is seldom mentioned in official literature, but is one of the main subjects of dissident literature. Stalin and his phantasmagoric system of camps are as vital to *samizdat* as patriotic war stories are to the Union of Writers.

Although there are notable and early exceptions such as Varlam Shalamov's tales, the camp theme seems to be more prominent in long novels than in short stories (Maximov, Solzhenitsyn). The military theme is not as restricted by genre. Most Russians still like reading about their Great Patriotic War in spite of its distance; I agree with Klaus Mehnert (author of *The Russians and Their Favorite Books*) and others—it makes them feel good. What about plot? Particularly among the dominant realist writers, the short story often tends toward the character sketch rather than the O. Henry-style plot construction. This, too, is traditional in most Russian literature. Who are the characters? Stories about country eccentrics, quiet rural heroes, strong old women, the "grabbers," and the conscious-stricken city bourgeoisie have been staples of Soviet literature at least since the early 1960s. Aitmatov, Iskander and other writers who describe non-Russian life in such regions as Kirghizia, Abkhazia, or among any of the many tribes from the Urals to far Siberia (Siberia is a particularly popular setting vaguely like our Wild West), also tend to find analogous kinds of "little" heroes. The true positive hero of the Stalin era is rare. The exception is in the official prize-winning novels; indeed, that hero is mainly a creature of the Union of Writers' authorities, such as Georgy Markov and other powerful secretaries who pen (or have ghost-written) multi-volume epics, dutifully bought and shelved by Party careerists and eagerly read by Soviet Petrushkas, e.g., Gogolian types who will read *anything* in front of them with great pleasure and no understanding. This is called "Secretariat Literature" by the cognoscenti. Of such writers Aksyonov writes:

> For them there is a higher system of royalties and for figuring the number of copies in an edition, i.e., they are able to get the maximum amount of money out of their books. Essentially free country dachas and other goodies are set aside for them by the Literary Fund, an organization founded over one hundred years ago with the idea of its noble founders that it was intended to help "writers who are have-nots and drinkers." Now everything is turned around. It's only with great trouble that the poor average writer can get a pitful loan that he must repay, while the richest and most prominent, that is, the secretaries, get solid nonrepayable stipends for moving, say several thousand rubles to move to a new apartment, to repair the garden benches at their dachas a few thousand. Not to mention the city apartments, secretarial comfort (in Moscow right now they are all moving into the street with the convincing name of Atheist Street).

Among the most valuable privileges of the Union's secretaries is absolute freedom from negative reviews anywhere in the press and the right to make regular Union-paid trips abroad. Aksyonov guesses there are about three hundred such Union of Writers' secretaries all over the country. A number of the authors Klaus Mehnert finds among the forty-eight most popular of the USSR are many of these secretaries. Mehnert is astoundingly naive about the authors—seeing almost no propaganda in them and their readers.

The main characters of nearly all of the writers—from country writers such as Victor Astafiev and Vasily Belov to "city writers" such as Nina Katerli or I. Grekova—do fight battles. They try to do things in the face of resistance, but it is seldom that their tests are anything more than the tests which everyday life and Soviet *byt* ("existence," the sum of things and customs in everyday life) put before them. They are ordinary people trying to do something hard—live. Their struggles are to get a larger apartment, to deal with an unwanted grandmother, to buy a TV, to butter up their boss, to hold a full-time job (for women) and still have to stand in lines to get basic foodstuffs or handle a drunken husband. Compared to the great character types and crucial tests of classic Russian literature (from Akaky Akakievich to Ivan Ilich), they are not universalized and their test is ordinary. It's as if *byt* were the central Russian problem and the main determinant of character.

The world of the characters is usually narrow. Soviet characters not only do not travel to different countries much, but their radius of action for a whole life is ordinarily very restricted. (The war or a camp may make an exception to this rule.) They seldom know what's happening outside their home, never mind in the world at large. And since they live at a fairly simple, subsistence level, basic housing and when they will eat meat are central issues. Modern civilization does not provide many tests. Characters do not have their lives complicated by such Western problems as sudden fortune, who to vote for at the next election, falling in love with one's psychotherapist, computer burn-out, or even moving to a new house out of state. Sex concerns them, of course, but even in 1984 it is never the subject of detailed thought, description, or fantasy. The works of Trifonov and Rasputin are characteristic of the Soviet approach, even though each writer has original touches. The sexual slap a provocative girl endures in Trifonov's story "Games at Dusk" is as close as a Soviet writer can get even to that famous whip in *First Love* (so beloved by the Japanese in their numberless translations of the Turgenev story).

It is not very well known in the West that form is almost as likely to get one banned by an editor or censor as content. This is absolutely true in the USSR, but even emigre Russian editors are on the whole conservative, traditional realists. Most victories over the censors, violations of the taboos, which Russian writers and readers boasted about in the sixties and seventies, were thematic victories. So-and-so said something that had never been said before, and it "got by" everyone. Since forbidden topics are myriad, the new truth, or portion of the truth, could be almost anything. Russian readers *lived* for this kind of breakthrough. They waited in line on Kalinin Prospect, Moscow Art Theater Lane, Kuznetsk Bridge or at the hundreds of kiosks for books or magazines that had—or were rumored to have—such new truths and semi-truths. However, the poet or prose writer who wanted to experiment with style alone was no less likely than the thematic heretic to get red ink in his face and bad comments on his work record.

Poets were harder to pin down, especially if they were optimistic, patriotic, could describe a drill-press, or did the usual stultifying nature descriptions. But they had to watch their language, their metaphors, and their allusions. Colloquialisms, especially the really new ones, ones young people loved, were dangerous; metaphors had better be simple and comprehensible—none of that Pasternak mumbo-jumbo; the encyclopedia of *Myths of the Peoples of the World* didn't get published until 1980-82, so too many allusions to classical gods and goddesses were out. In short, nothing too "imaginative," nothing too hard—for those are signs of "bad" verse, poetry incomprehensible to the masses.

As for prose, there the form-censors no doubt felt surer of themselves. In many ways Sokolov's *A School for Fools* is an angry compendium of precisely all the things that cannot be done with form in the Soviet Union. Stream-of-consciousness is out; after all, they've had Joyce on the pillory for sixty years, the chief demon of Modernism (whatever that is). Proustian detail and self-analysis is impossible. The use of the grotesque and fantastic must be held to a bare minimum, even if the editor is a liberal; Kafka was not banned for so many decades on a whim. Chronology cannot be too disorderly, let alone obliterated; it is the first step to easy comprehension by metro riders, pensioners, and collective farm workers of average education. Therefore departures from normal chronology must be comprehensible without much page turning, and even then it is allowed mainly to writers over seventy who have proved their loyalty, old men like Kataev, who had voted to throw Pasternak out of the Union of Writers in 1958, and dutifully attacked Solzhenitsyn a decade or so later.

The mode of fantasy must be used with great caution. For example, the mild Bulgakovian fantasy which Nina Katerli uses in some of her stories, such as "The Barsukov Triangle," makes them unpublishable in the Soviet Union—even though in most respects she writes such realistic stories that I would recommend precisely her work to anyone who wants to know what city life is like in the USSR (she has published in various journals and has issued one small book). The fact is that both in terms of long Russian convention and the forced marching called Socialist Realism, the writers fall into a tradition. Realism is a tradition which most Russian writers naturally find congenial, but one which is positively enforced by Union of Writers' privileges (special housing, special food, special medicine, and special vacations—not to mention medals) and negatively enforced by KGB sanctions (from "talks" and non-publication to barbed wire and guard dogs).

Language is another area of form where the censorship plays a role. Uniformity of style is another major goal of the censors and the writers unwittingly have done much to accommodate them. Here we get to a major and interesting debate. Ideally the editor and censor would like the diction to be unnoticed and unnoticeable. The language of everyday life; i.e., newspapers, Party decrees and informational bulletins, and the classics of the past, from Chernyshevsky to Furmanov and Belinsky to Lenin, should be the models. Aside from warning articles in periodicals—*The Literary Gazette, Questions of Literature,* and even *Russian Language in School,* there was a powerful weapon used by authorities to insure linguistic conformity—dictionaries. While it is true the Soviets produced the largest multi-volume dictionary of the Russian literary language (17 vols., 1950-65) and that other lexicographers like Ushakov did brilliant work, neither set was common on writers' desks after Stalin. Writers, like most Russians, instead used the acceptable 50,000 words of the dull, dreadful, ubiquitous *Ozhegov Dictionary,* which wordsmiths such as Nabokov have justly abused. For limited minds, the perfect Sovietese and nugatory definitions of numberless Ozhegovs were the ideal weapon. When the country prose craze started (since most writers didn't know much about real country speech), the good old *Dahl Dictionary* (1840s) was reprinted a number of times—naturally not its best editions supplemented by Baudouin de Courtenay, but the bowdlerized ones. Even cut, it is a good lexicon which many serious writers have praised, but it is a century old (thus certain dangerous modern concepts and usages are safely absent), and the much more up-to-date four-volume Ushakov became very hard to get.

The Soviet Union is the perfect vertical corporation; it controls everything needed to write, from—depending on the decrees of the latest Party Congress or Union of Writers' Plenum—the subjects that need to be written about to the words that the authors should use. For example, one of the main features of the early works of Vasily Aksyonov was the startling new language. Stories such as his "A Ticket to the Stars" and "Halfway to the Moon" were the Soviet equivalent to *The Catcher in the Rye* and more. He wrote very much the way the young generation actually talked. Pieces such as "Surplussed Barrelware" drove sedentary translators to despair. And he continued to use that diction, indeed to expand it, especially when the West became his subject matter. Even when he was popular, he got the low payments that dubious rebels get. He was lucky that he had an editor who gave him fairly free rein (good old Kataev at *Youth*) and that he came on the scene during one of those lax periods that misled everyone, at least until the tanks entered Prague. But long before this, Aksyonov had Khrushchev yelling at him in pubilc, and as time passed he noticed his money was gone and that he wasn't getting much published (eleven years of enforced silence), and in the end, when he finally published the works that reflected his true, completely unfettered language (he recalls he had to "order" his writing hand to be free), such as his major novel *The Burn,* it was 1980 and his book was published not in Moscow but in Michigan. The censors had no work to do on this because the KGB and Union of Writers worked in tandem to get him out of the Union and out of the country. Quite apart from its subject matter, the novel could never have been published there on grounds of (1) language, (2) structure and chronology, and (3) the use of fantasy in characterization. One could do a similar analysis of Bitov's *Pushkin House* from the formal point of view and show that it too had to appear whole only abroad almost as much because of its form, beautifully symmetrical, but "too literary" and perhaps intended as camouflage, as for its content, which was relatively uninflammatory except for a few discussions about the aristocracy and Russian history in the year 1937. And finally, Bitov shares another sin with Aksyonov and a handful of other writers who at least began their careers under the censors—you can tell his unique style immediately. This can be said of Trifonov and a few others, but it is very unusual.

Of course, if we talk about *another* kind of language—*mat,* dirty language—the case is simple. Soviet editors never print dirty words. When Solzhenitsyn got *One Day* published, the theme was approved by everyone from Tvardovsky to Khrushchev, but the language was another matter. No matter how mild and realistic the language was, he had to clean it up with the help of friendly editors. And since he wanted to belong and be published in the journal *Novyi Mir,* he did; but even so, the relatively gentle terms left in caused great shock and debate. It was the beginning of a new kind of language. Dictionaries of camp language began to appear all over in the West, and some texts were smuggled out of the Soviet Union. One former prisoner, now at Harvard, was already working on thousands of cards for a future dictionary of "non-normative" Russian. All the words that show realia which in theory do not exist, all the regional vernaculars, all the forbidden words will be in it.

In the case of a writer who thrives on dirty words, whose natural narrative idiom is the unrestrained, colorful "filthy" language of the camp inmate, the *zek,* such a writer would never bother to submit his novels or stories anywhere—the first page would do him in. Yuz Aleshkovsky, whose *Kangaroo* is coming out this fall, is the best of these. The funny thing is that when just such a writer left Russia, he ran into the same puritanism here. Most emigre Russians fully agree swear words should not be printed, that here too the press should be pure. Thus, for example, Andrei Sedykh, chief editor of America's main Russian newspaper, *Novoe Russkoe Slovo,* wrote Ardis a letter rejecting excerpts from Aksyonov's *The Burn* on the grounds that they contained "so much coarseness, so much vulgarity, that I cannot use them." And when Aleshkovsky published something in Maximov's *Continent* (Paris), the editors censored his language. When the New York emigre publisher Russica published Eduard Limonov's Russian *It's Me, Eddie,* they put the name *Index Publishers* on the book so that they would not get the blame for the bad language and sexual descriptions. Parts of the controversial novel had previously appeared in the journal *The Ark.* Its translation by Random House was largely ignored by reviewers, but Limonov got emigre periodicals so enraged that his very name was blacklisted by some.

Form, language—what does this leave us with? With one area of acceptable innovation. As already observed, when country prose came in, the pale, polluted bureaucratese and the hackneyed plain vocabulary of the socialist realist classics were supplanted by something which was at least *realistic.* Indeed, the very fact that it was realistic and from the "folk" (*narod*) made it acceptable in principle. So for the first time in decades, the rich dialects of many areas of the Soviet Union were reflected in literature. Abramov, Belov, Mozhaev, Shukshin, Astafiev, Zalygin and many others—to widely varying degrees—did bring something new to the language of literature which bears Glavlit's stamp on every galley. This is one of the reasons Solzhenitsyn has repeatedly praised the country writers, although there are also ideological bases to his approval. Furthermore, Solzhenitsyn himself writes in a language consciously constructed to be "truly Russian" and avoids those city-Party-bureaucratic cliches. As far as it goes this is good. It does let fresh air in. It's good that so many writers rediscovered the old *Dahl Dictionary* with the thousands of colloquial and dialectical words and idioms the scholar recorded. When the writers actually knew the country and didn't *overdo* this new vocabulary mercilessly, it was not a bad thing to happen. Therefore, the editors allowed the lexicon to expand.

What, ultimately, did this get them? Well, the bad thing that it got them is provincialism—and this is still true today. Imagine that a large number of the important American novelists wrote exclusively on the basis of Mark Twain's dialects and used an 1840 dictionary for color and originality. This is not as bad as the Russian situation, but it is a rough analogy. While piling on the demotic—in the course of which country writers describe every old wooden utensil that ever existed—they often forget such things as interest, characterization, plot and so on. Writing degenerates into the kind of ethnographic reportage that typifies such dead Nobel classics as Reymont's *Peasants,* or into the dull historical instruction sheets that make up much of Solzhenitsyn's never-ending *Red Wheel* ("Stolypin and His Reforms" is even printed in small type and accompanied by the author's suggestion that the less serious reader skip the 60 pages).

So our final answer is clearly, yes, form is a fact in censorship. The Soviet writer can tinker with chronological blocks or use the Archangel peasants' quaint words for turnips or boot-liners, but he cannot invent truly new forms. The Russian author can't do any of the formal experiments, good or bad, laughable or interesting, boring or inspiring that typify contemporary Western writers such as Pynchon, Elkin, Barth, Spackman, or Gilbert Sorrentino.

Once again it is worth noting that many of the same attitudes toward formal innovations are widespread in the Russian emigration, too. In emigre journals and publishing houses traditional realism is predominant. There is not much question of experimentation in the Russian books published by Possev (Germany) or YMCA (France); and the journals with the longest lives and most subscribers, *Continent* and *Time and Us* (New York), for the most part publish poetry, stories and novels whose form (but *not* content) would be acceptable in the USSR. Language restrictions, except for swear words, are much less obvious than in the USSR; but in any case most writers follow the standards they were brought up on. Journals more open to risk in form and theme do not last long—e. g., *The Ark, Echo* (Paris). The great majority of prose and poetry published both in Russian and in English, even by Ardis, which has a reputation for being "modernist" or "elitist," has been traditionally realistic and unexperimental.

What kind of writer is officially approved and widely read in the USSR? I regret to say that in *The Russians and Their Favorite Books* Klaus Mehnert is generally right about the reading tastes and habits of the average Russian intellectual. He lists a "top 24" and 24 runners-up. Among the most read (and least translated) is Sergei Zalygin. Zalygin is also very old and reliable, and he is a Union secretary who signed the required letters attacking liberal writers, so he is able to get away with some devices and subjects off-limits to young writers, including the use of fantasy, positive pictures of old-fashioned characters and superstition. The sentimentalism and Sucaryl levels are high. I present below the recent birthday greeting to him from the Union of Writers

Secretariat. It will give the reader a clear idea of official style and the sorts of things which are of value to the officers of the main writing organization.

We Congratulate on His Jubilee: Sergei Zalygin, 70 Years Old

The Secretariat of the Directorate of the Union of Writers of the USSR has sent the following greeting to Sergei Pavlovich Zalygin: "We heartily congratulate you, a notable Soviet Writer, on your seventieth birthday.

You entered literature with rich life and workplace experience. You wrote your first works while working as a hydrological engineer, as a participant in the great constructive work spreading out across the wide-open spaces of Siberia.

In 45 years of creative activity you have contributed a great block of material to the development of our literature. In your work, devoted to the most important events in the life of the Soviet people, up-to-date questions about modernity, and to the heroic pages of the history of our state, you understand the big social, moral problems, with talent you reveal the characters and fates of the Soviet people—laborers of the city and the country. Your books are extremely popular among the readers of our country; they are published in the languages of the peoples of the USSR, in foreign languages.

Your original talent shone brightly in such works as the novels *Altai Paths, Salt Valley, The Commission, The South American Variant*, and the novella *On the Irtysh*. You are now publishing the new novel *After the Storm*. Your works serve to educate Soviet people in the spirit of patriotism, socialist internationalism, and humanism. For the novel *Salt Valley* you were awarded the State Prize of the USSR.

To your pen belong publicistic works devoted to the defense of our native nature, the sensible use of its riches. Your literary scholarship and critical works—*An Interview with Myself*, the essay on A. P. Chekhov, "My Past," and others—were met with interest.

You carry on active social activity as a member of the Directorate of the Union of Writers of the USSR, a Secretary of the Union of Writers of the RSFSR, the Chairman of the Council on Latvian Literature of the Union of Writers of the USSR.

For services in the development of Soviet literature you have been awarded the Order of Lenin, two Orders of the Workers' Red Star, and other medals. You have been granted the title of Deserving Activist of Culture of the Latvian SSR.

We wish you, dear Sergei Pavlovich, good health and new creative successes."

Among the others whom Mehnert (correctly, I think) puts at the top in print-runs are a few generally interesting writers, including Trifonov, Shukshin, Abramov, and Rasputin. The cult of Shukshin continues, probably more because of his subjects and his movie efforts than his writing. The Soviets continue to publish him very actively in many forms for readers of all ages. Trifonov is a far superior writer with a far better sense of literary traditions, but publications since his death have been few and far between. Even during his lifetime he was published less than more favored writers such as Abramov and Shukshin. If we very skeptically (Soviet statistics are seldom reliable) accept the figures Mehnert cites from the *Yearbook of Soviet Books* from 1967-79, all of Trifonov's books had run to 1,747,000 copies, plus one appearance in the cheap, high-run *Newspaper Novel* (c. 2,000,000 copies). In comparison Fyodor Abramov's copies run to 2,629,000 plus two appearances (i.e., another 4,000,000) in the *Newspaper Novel,* and Shukshin to 2,744,000 plus one *Newspaper Novel* appearance. (Contrast the "Secretariat Literature" which Aksyonov described. The non-writer who is First Secretary of the Union of Writers, Georgy Markov, had 5,162,000 books, plus 8,000,000 more in four *Newspaper Novel* publications.) A variety of facts leads us to conclude that Trifonov, who was easily the most controversial and liberal of this group, and who made enemies among the authorities, has fallen even further behind Abramov or Shukshin since his death.

Rasputin is the only respectable writer left among the top 24 (though Grekova and Iskander are in the next 24). This leaves us with only one writer—Rasputin—who still publishes exclusively in the USSR, who is largely approved by the authorities, who has managed to produce four important novels, not only original and independent for the Soviet Union, but also good enough to be translated into English and other languages largely on their own merit (I say "largely" because at the 1977 book fair VAAP made a concerted effort to sell rights to Rasputin, and the American publishing house Macmillan, which already had close Soviet publishing ties, bought all of his best work). Born in the fateful and fatal year of 1937, he is the youngest of the Soviet classics writing now and also the youngest among Mehnert's "top 24," having sold about 1,427,000 copies between 1969-79, plus another four million copies with two novels in that influential *Newspaper Novel.* His novels, especially *Farewell to Matyora* (1976), are better than his stories. Two unusual facts about this quiet fellow are worth noting. In March 1980 he was viciously beaten in Novosibirsk, apparently for his jeans; he underwent two operations, and for a while his future was in doubt. But in 1982 he published a new story in *Our Contemporary,* currently one of the most powerful literary journals, one with a general reputation for conservatism. He is the best living Soviet writer who (1) seems never to have had trouble with the official establishment, and (2) has not been corrupted by the official machine. He has never voted to throw anyone out of the Union of Writers, or even signed collective letters attacking writers in disfavor. He has never made political statements (condemning, say, nuclear weapons or American leaders). Finally, unlike Aitmatov, he has never provided the kinds of toe-the-line interviews or essays which are demanded of every well-known Soviet writer. What we are to make of this, it is difficult to say. Soviet Russian literature has always had intriguing anomalies which suggest the ultimate strength of human spirit. But I fear the future does not belong to the likes of Rasputin, who has one thing in his favor—he lives in Siberia.

Predicting the immediate future of Russian literature is rather perilous, especially as it relates to the authors who publish only in the Soviet Union. As has been the case since the late fifties, prose is more important than poetry. While Iskander and Andrei Bitov may have their best work ahead of them, now, and for the next few years, most of the interesting activity will be among writers abroad—both traditionalists and "others." I purposely do not say "experimentalists," because the most obvious figures who are commonly pigeon-holed here—Sasha Sokolov, Andrei Sinyavsky—are, for all their innovations, traditionalists in the best sense of the word. Like other experimenter-traditionalists, Sinyavsky and Sokolov have the advantage of almost total ignorance of the ideas educated people associate with Joyce and others in the period around World War One. Otherwise, much of their fiction would be irrelevant. In this case Russia's isolationism actually had a valuable side. The newest emigres have done much to evaluate themselves, not infrequently concluding the best writer is—"X"—i.e., whoever is writing. In any case, the achievements and prospects of the "Third Wave" have been analyzed in detail by the poets, prose writers, critics, and editors themselves.

Not a few Russian writers believe that contemporary Russian literature is superior to American or other Western literatures. At the same time, by means of inflated figures for writers such as Jack London, Dreiser, and Mayne Reid (!), the Soviets' regular line is that they print more American literature than we do Russian. However, the fact is that both nineteenth- and twentieth-century Russian writers are more easily available in English-speaking countries than

American literature is in the USSR. (Indeed, *Russian* books are more widely available here.) See, for example, M. Friedberg, *A Helsinki Record: The Availability of Soviet Russian Literature in the United States* (New York: Helsinki Watch Committee, 1980). This report is just the beginning of what might be said.

The Soviet argument that Russian literature is superior to Western writing has been used, in an inverted form, by emigre Russians as well, ranging from the barely comprehensible Lev Navrozov to some well-known writers. The editor of the most influential Russian journal abroad, Vladimir Maximov, argues this case in a recent interview. Since none of the Russian writers with whom I am acquainted know very much about American literature, this is a curious topic for debate. I suspect the nationalistic "Russia, Christ of Nations" notion from Solzhenitsyn's Harvard Speech is at the core of much emigre thinking and writing. I know what expletive Nadezhda Mandelstam would use to describe such militant know-nothingness. Neither Soviets nor Russian emigres know much (if anything) of such unconventional English-language writers as Thomas Pynchon, Stanley Elkin, W. M. Spackman, Joan Didion, Donald Barthelme, Edmund White, Cynthia Ozick, John Hawkes, Tom Robbins, or Gilbert Sorrentino, to name only a few writers whose works will not often be translated by the world's most literature-loving nation. More revealing is that Russian writing, no matter where it is done, is largely ignorant of and less accomplished than our own so-called realistic or traditional writers in English. Thus, the older generation's Elizabeth Bowen, Anthony Powell and Kay Boyle, or such contemporary "realistic" writers as Fowles, Oates, Paley, Bellow, Roth, Updike, Stone, Irving, Heller, Rossner and Beattie do far more that is original than most of their Russian contemporaries. It is very simple. They were brought up as free people and learned their art in freedom. But too many Russians want to believe that even if they have become disillusioned with the totalitarianism they once helped, they are still superior to the West morally and artistically.

Soviet knowledge of significant American and British writers is woefully poor. Remember *Moby Dick* was not translated into Russian until the late 1950s, nor *Pride and Prejudice* until the same period. The same is true of Russians in the emigration. A few read a few new things, but essentially my experience is that no Russians know the authors above or the many others who could be added. Indeed, their language ability keeps them from finding out about the new literary milieu (outside of a few New York aspects). Thus, technically

156

Solzhenitsyn is free now; but he is somehow forced to surround himself with wire, to limit his language, to remain—as he has been for twenty years—the singer of the camp and war, with the worried psychology of a prisoner. In spite of their ignorance, like most of their well-known Eastern European colleagues, such as Kundera, they continue to believe they live in the future (because of their suffering under Marxism which is supposed to foreshadow ours), unaware that in fact they are living in the past, both in their irony-filled works and in their inability to recognize that Russia and the East *are* throwbacks to less enlightened ages. In the next few years we will find many more re-readable books from Aksyonov, Voinovich, Brodsky and others than we will see from the USSR. Many emigre journals are amateurish and have short lives, but *Continent* will continue to be more varied, diverting and lively than *Novyi mir.* Rozanova's resolutely independent journal *Syntax* will continue to be worthy opposition to the politics of *Continent.* All the early signs are that in spite of the increasing difficulty of finding truly good material, Georgy Vladimov will improve *Facets* markedly.

While emigre periodicals have their troubles, in the last few years the entire Soviet literary press has become a shambles. "Colonial novels" like Alexander Prokhanov's immortal *A Tree in Kabul* are not only given serious attention, but even get translated and discussed in the propaganda journal *Soviet Literature. Novyi mir* is lucky to print something good once a year; without Trifonov *Friendship of the Peoples* is dead; *Our Contemporary* does a little better, but the editors' applause for the government is a little louder than required. The newspapers are a joke. *The Literary Gazette* used to be interesting sometimes; but now the hysterical tone has spread to every column, and even the fabrications are done so idiotically that it's no longer worthwhile reading them for fun. The reports on various plenums and directorate meetings are beyond all imagination. The gobbledigookish messages these plenums sent (printed) to Brezhnev in his last couple of years were at least a polite goodbye, usually extolling his leadership of them and his skimpy (no doubt ghostwritten) Lenin Prize winning memoirs. Under Andropov and Chernenko the vigilance campaigns have become more shrill and ominous, and the directorate reports more servile as they explain how they discussed Central Committee Resolutions such as "On the Further Improvement of Ideological, Politico-Educational Work" (*Literary Russia,* June 1, 1979) or the especially menacing "On Creative Connections between Literary-Artistic Journals and the Practice of Communist Construction" (*The

Literary Gazette, August 18, 1982). Admonitory dicta from the leaders are printed in set-off boxes, like Andropov's in *The Literary Gazette* (July 13, 1983): "The main method of influence on artistic works must be Marxist-Leninist criticism, active, sensitive, attentive and at the same time unrelenting towards ideologically alien or professionally weak works."

The names of the authors and the subjects of the works (*Lenin in Paris*) which have been nominated for Lenin Prizes, State Prizes and so on have become progressively more obscure and ludicrous. Lucrative but never prestigious west of Minsk, the awards have been steadily debased by cut-throat Union of Writers officials and a new generation of toadies. Those from the so-called "People's Republics" are multiplying. The example of Chingiz Aitmatov, who has something to recommend him as a writer, has had very deleterious effects. He is at least a writer *and* a mouthpiece (he also helped pillory Solzhenitsyn); the new ones are only mouthpieces. Copies of Chakovsky and Bondarev will continue to be bought and read by the millions, and no doubt Russian readers will snap up more millions of the *Newspaper Novel* (each writer has appeared there six times, i.e., 12,000,000 copies), which reprints their novels. Ivanov will be just as popular, along with Pikul, Alexeev, and even poor, dumb—but mean—Stadnyuk. Semyonov's novels will continue to be serialized on Soviet television and seen by as many as 150 million viewers. There is no question that in a related vein John Le Carré's *Tinker, Tailor, Soldier, Spy* was immensely superior as a novel and on the television screen. For that matter even if we get past the hard-core buyers of books to TV and TV films the Russian blockbusters are infinitely inferior to *Holocaust, Roots,* or even the television version of such novels as *Rich Man, Poor Man* and *Centennial.* Good, professional middle-rank writers such as Shaw and Michener have never existed in Russia.

One final curiosity about the isolationism and paranoia of Soviet literary officials: new books are monitored with special care, but older books—the entire realm of second-hand sales—are now also subject to controls so strict they are hard to imagine. Thus printed instructions to all second-hand book trade units (all government owned and run) naturally prohibit the sale of any book on the "Consolidated List of Books Subject to Exclusion from Libraries and Retail Stores," but they also establish a hierarchy of stamps to mark each book to show what special category of person can *see* it.

Soviet Russian culture is impoverished in all areas, and this is one of the explanations for the apparent book-hunger we have all heard so much about. The paper shortage is always cited by authorities as the reason for not having big editions of someone like Akhmadulina, but this is a transparent lie. They have plenty of their "good" high-acid content, sixty-pound paper for political literature and "Secretariat Literature." The Soviets' own definitions and statistics show them having an annual consumption of "printing and writing" paper, per capita (in kilograms), of 5,117 (USSR) vs. 65,603 (USA) and 31,794 (UK). No doubt this is intentional in its relation to book-hunger and their UNESCO statistics on literary titles are sheer fabrications. If we consider the massive world of private and small press printing, I am sure that there is more reading of good literature here than there (aside from the low quality which Mehnert proves), and that more new literary journals and books appear annually in America, not to mention England, even though many are unrecorded, since we have no real national yearbooks. Of course the Soviet paper problem has its funny side. When the KGB tried to persuade the poet Joseph Brodsky to cooperate with them in the sixties, the main reward they offered was that a book of his poems would be "printed on good Finnish paper."

1984